Links of the Chain

Will James Harnack

Published by Will James Harnack, 2020.

LINKS OF THE CHAIN

First edition. December 3, 2020.

Copyright © 2020 Will James Harnack.

ISBN: 978-1393289937

Written by Will James Harnack.

Table of Contents

For my Parents and Grandparents

LINKS OF THE CHAIN

"HARNACK CAPTURES THE special quality of life in Wisconsin's North Country.... If the writing is regional, it's in the broad spectrum of such writing that includes authors such as Sherwood Anderson."
—Robert W. Wells, Milwaukee Journal Book Editor

"YOU ARE DOING IN PRINT what it seems Seurat and Renoir did in oil on canvas: vibrating with the stuff of everyday living and feeling but in your case with a lively sense of value."
—Lester Mondale, Philosopher (brother of Walter Mondale)

"POIGNANT, REMINDED me of my own life. The mystique of the Northwoods."
—Antler, Milwaukee Poet Laureate, Recipient of the Walt Whitman Award

1

"In my mind, there's this mythical place in America where the story-teller lives, and he tells stories based on this place and on people who've passed through it. I've never been there, but we all know it's there."

—J.R. Robertson

"There are no truths. Only stories."

—Thomas King, Native American Writer, from *Green Grass, Running Water*

Preface

Like grapevines and cocoa beans that reflect through their flavor the soil and water in which they grow, some places become part of a person's emotional and mental fabric. The evocative, elegiac stories comprising *Links of the Chain* present the human threads woven through a small northern Wisconsin town. The tales span decades, with characters disappearing and re-emerging, forging, severing or repairing links, bound together by the vibrations and ethos of the remote northern woods and water. Reading the book feels at turns like watching the flickering 8mm films of home movies, flashes of a familiar past linking up with the present. Sherman, Wisconsin is the stage, the foundation and steadfast witness to life, death, loss, love and memory. — Rebecca Murphy, Ludington, MI

Vacation

M y fishing rod whips forward and the lure is suspended in the air, against the blue sky in a momentary grace that is also remembered: a reference for everything in time not as beautiful as the sight of a silver lure in the sun. Then it is gone, under the waves while my vision floats on the gently undulating surface. I stand firmly on the old pier, while my body floats with my vision, as it is, as it was—

My bait nears the boat: wiggly and shiny and clean. Then it hangs from my rod, barren. I put my arm back and throw out again with my thumb riding the spool of wet line, as Grandpa taught me. It glistens in the sun and dives into the water. I stop the spinning with my thumb. Then I see just the waves and the shore and sky while I hope I will feel the tug and not be scared because I never felt it before. Reeling in, I hear Grandpa's words and watch an osprey dive so easily for a fish it sees from the air. I wonder why I cannot see the fish like that.

"Yes, I talk a lot about the past. It's because it is all I know. I don't know what things will be like in fifty years—or even tomorrow. So why talk about it? The future's not yours like the past is. And now is just the tail end of what's come before. Like reeling in that bait of yours and coming to the end. When you hook a big one it's gonna be the fight you will remember, what you'll tell everyone about. Not the helpless fish lying there in the boat on your way home."

—but not realizing the bait is in already, my hand suddenly stops turning. I feel the forest thick with quiet behind me as I again send the lure into the sky and lake. If a fish strikes it will surprise me, for I am not thinking about the fish. My vision rests over the water on the far shore: the small resort I can barely see, but knowing the details well, I see much more. Just as I know that the dense solid green of the shoreline consists of individual trees of distinct form, known and unchanged since childhood, like the clear blue sky of now which we swam under, then, and later—

She: Can I go mother, please (I watching, hoping)

Well yes I suppose you can, so we take their truck because she said we could. Mary tunes the radio and I feel a little scared and proud because I never drove a standard shift before. When we get to town she points out things and tells me stories and I'm realizing how I didn't know the town like I thought I did. She yells to some girls who stand in front of the A & W and they giggle and wave and talk among themselves. As we ride down the highway she tells me how it has not rained since July fourth and her parents are worried. They will have to irrigate the potato farm from the lake and I'm thinking how the fine dust coated her bare feet when we walked along the road that day. I drive slowly onto the rutted entrance of the drive-in and glance at her soft brown hair that smells of sunshine and lakewater and my heart burns because she looks so happy and proud and I feel just that way too. I pay the girl in the booth the four dollars my father gave me. She is turning up the radio because California Girls[1] is playing and it's summer. Rumbling to the row before the refreshment stand, I turn and drive up the mound of gravel until the car is inclined upward to face the great white screen. The sun, a large orange ball afloat in the heat, is setting behind the screen, sinking into an August-dry field of oats. We wait until it becomes cooler and then close the windows. The mosquitoes are getting thick, too.

And I throw out again. Mountainous thunderheads have formed over the western horizon. I am aware of their brooding darkness, conscious of the rain they will deliver soon, as I watch a muskrat swim steadily along the shore. It is our shoreline, as it has been since Grandpa bought it from The Continental Lumber Company in 1932. Conti-

---

1.   *https://youtu.be/fmIsdMWzdaE*

nental Lumber acquired it (the legal abstract continued) by sale from a Mr. A. K. Lepchek, who bought it from the U.S. Government, who took it, the original forty-acre lake plot, through force or treaty or both, from the Chippewa Indians and whoever saw it and wanted it before them. And me at the end of this line of acquisition, sale, repudiation, and inheritance of this unchanging woods. The deeds are filed in a drawer in town. Still, the land remains oblivious to it; as uncaring of laws and files as it was before there were laws and files and paper. I hear the trees laugh in pine-whisper humor at it all. No, it was never owned; I do not own. Cannot except as Grandpa did, through love and respect and reverence for its order. He owned this forest, not because he found it or because he purchased it or even because he ordered it, but because he loved it and respected it.

"Hello?"

I am startled but somehow not surprised that the thick, silent forest speaks. My lonely thoughts require it somehow—welcome it. As I turn I begin to reel in again because the hand had stopped like everything in the moment of the spoken word.

"Hello," I respond.

"Don't be afraid of Bear."

Bear, I notice, is a giant St. Bernard, standing nearly as tall as the girl who speaks. She emerges from the woods alone, a young teenager.

"You startled me. I haven't seen a person in days."

"We're walking around the lake," she explains.

I remember once I had tried very hard to circumambulate the entire lake without success. My bait now hangs clean and I click the lock and remove my thumb.

"Are you from the resort?"

"Yeah, if you can call it that. So boring! Everyone's in our cabin playing cards."

The smile across my face feels good. "Well, I'm glad to have company. But I don't think you'll be able to walk around the lake. Another hundred yards you'll hit impenetrable swamp."

The dog sits enormously, listening to me.

"Well, I'm going to try. Goodbye." A quick smile and she begins to walk, the domestic beast following.

"Wait."

I am off the pier, leaning the rod against a tree and following the dog. I need human company a bit longer, I think; knowing I want to know what she can now tell. I am also interested to see what my unexpected guest will do when she encounters the marsh.

"Can't you fish and go swimming across the lake?" I ask, remembering the many days spent there during vacations, laughing under sunny skies.

"I hate to fish. And there's no one to swim with. Besides, the bottom is mucky."

I dive through the cold water until my hand touches the soft, cool sediment, so rich and fertile in its decay. A little scary in the dark depth. But on the surface again she is peacefully sunning on the diving raft, unaware; I also dismiss it.

The girl is talking. "Last year we went to a place in Elksburg where I could water ski. Daddy wouldn't take us back 'cause he didn't catch a muskie."

—the speedboat I'm proud to drive and she skiing behind. I glance over my shoulder to see her skim over the water, jumping off the swells, hair blowing back in the wind. I am leading her, amazed how the lake shrinks from the increased speed. It feels a little heretical and I wonder if Grandpa is watching.

"They had a speedboat for skiing," I say. She says the steering cord is broke and its an ancient relic, anyway. We are walking on the path along the lake which I always believed Grandpa created. It is actually a deer path. They let Grandpa (and us) use it.

It is beginning to rain. I do not say anything because I have already tried to dilute the enthusiasm of her brave plans. She seems so intent.

Here is the swamp. I will watch her.

And I watch her. (The dog watches too, standing in front of me.) She stops and looks at it: the problem. Then she looks down to take it step by step. She finds an elevated ground, only to sink as her tennis shoe fills with water. I know how that feels. Then she tries another way and still another.

And I think, as I could not have then: we can't enter and pass through the swamp: that devious portion of terrestrial earth where life evolved, where man appeared and which will be the last place he takes a stand with his money, his machines, and his greed. That transition between earth and water, water to earth, is not conducive to our race which must either stand or sink. When we perish, if we perish, it will be after we take on the swamps and win. With luck, we will lose. Luck, that is, if it can't be something better—something from our ancestral past, maybe, when we still loved and venerated this land.

I see the girl's determination and feel good to have the security of these lowlands. She stands quietly, giving up. Then she turns and, noticing she stands between me and the bog, chooses me.

"You own all this?"

"Yes. Yes, I do. Come on. Let me drive you back around. It's going to pour soon."

I turn and walk back along the deer path, now in the lead, the beast still obedient in the middle.

"This was my grandfather's land. It now belongs to me. I haven't been here... in a few years."

"How come there aren't more cottages?"

"Well, for one thing, we're not on the Chain. We're on the edge of the National Forest—the edge of what's left of the true wilderness up here. There are some soggy lowlands, as you just found out." I grin. "Also, like you, many people don't like our mucky bottom."

"You like it here?"

"I like it."

Although I am lonely. I wouldn't mind if she came to swim off my pier—it's a bit more sandy than at the resort. No, that would be lonely for her. She needs that which young life finds so simply complex and intriguing—other young life. With age one forgets (or over-remembers until memory's colors mix into an imageless hue?) how to experience the moment with such innocent skill.

"Where are you from?" I ask.

"Rockford, Illinois. It's very dull."

"Have a boyfriend?"

"Just Mark."

We are at my cabin. I will not pursue it, not believe in what is gone. She will go on many more vacations before Mark and the others become precious re-creations of image upon image in endless and uncontrolled stagnation, resigning each to be remembered and known, simultaneously, as in one vast canvas. Then maybe we could talk about it. Now, I will drive her back across the lake, back in time also, to another's home where she waited and wrote to me and stopped writing. My palms begin to perspire as they will when the pure possibility exists of the inevitable present negating that which you foolishly believe the past to still be.

The girl sits beside me, and the dog fills the back seat. She turns on the radio and, finding just one station that isn't to her satisfaction, clicks it off. The close trees stream by, our gate passes, and we drive the well known dirt road for three miles before the blacktop begins. Soon we are on the Chain Road passing cottages built in hundred yard intervals.

"This is the only way to get around our lake."

"What lake is that?"

"Deer. Part of the Chain."

Fishermen are hurriedly bringing in their boats to escape the rain. The girl watches with interest. We pass three youths walking down the road, seemingly oblivious to the downpour. I know where she will try to go tomorrow.

The turnoff leading to the resort is near. The question moves to my lips.

"I used to drive this way, frequently. There was a girl who lived up in the resort house. About my age, brown hair..."

"You must mean Mary Ann. She dyes her hair blonde."

"Oh. Yes. She still lives there?"

"I guess. 'Cept she's leaving in October I hear." The girl watches me now. "Just got married."

I am feigning disinterest, but she knows she's got me.

"She talked my ear off this morning. She had a baby—a girl. I could hear it hollerin' up in the house." She pauses watching me. "I don't think the real father hung around long. The kid's got a new dad it seems, in the Army. They're moving to... Germany I think she said."

Yes, I knew it. It was expected. It was real but it became a dream. Or maybe it was a dream that has become real. It doesn't matter, the words don't really matter. The past is dead and maybe the present is too. I won't know until much later, if at all. But it is done for me, has been without my knowing consent. They can just love, trying to defeat time and its *it was* also.

I think: After all this, though, a paradox, somehow it lives; alive inside me and it is pure like nothing else. And something new: the thinking, the knowing of memory.

"I knew her once," I say.

We pass the familiar wood sign that reads, "The Birches." Then we are there and I stop the car beside the small guest cabin (which we had stained one fine afternoon—the wood still well preserved (*ah, I think now, was that meant to be a chore to keep her away from me?*). The big house stands on the hill, unchanged, in the now heavy rain.

"Were you in love with her?"

I glance at the girl. She asks this without embarrassment or sarcasm or shame or anything except simple interest, a conclusion to a simple story she has built in her mind of this small encounter.

I look up the hill. And I cannot answer simply. I could have then and I do not know why I can't now.

"All I know is how it felt—how I remember it feeling. It was very, very good and it was easy, but—"

But the girl and her dog are gone already and the door to the little cabin closing. She is, no doubt, telling her parents that she walked around the lake and didn't meet anyone. They are too busy playing cards and drinking to really hear her.

My foot presses the accelerator before my mind can work. I will go back to my cabin now. I will sit and try to write it down. And I will give up, returning to the far easier task of working on an academic paper on Turgenev, a task that exists in another world. I will read and then fish and saw the birch logs. Over dinner I'll listen to *Nashville Skyline* on the old record player. Perhaps in the fresh morning I will take a walk along Grandpa's old now fallen fence line. I did that one August afternoon with Grandpa when I was a boy.

Then it is Sunday. I begin closing the cabin in the manner and order he established which cannot change. My hands work at turning the valves of the old water system. I secure the heavy pine shutters. I pull the boat up on the trailer Grandpa designed for that task. When it is done I go to bed, to the echo of a single loon crying on the lake. I am up early and climb the hill to my car. And I am driving. I pass the gate and do not close it. I drive north through town and then through another town. I am driving along the endless, driftwood-strewn shore of Lake Michigan when I see an awkward, sunbleached rectangular monument: the screen of a drive-in theater. Beside the soaring pines, it intrudes like a huge signboard, only blank and messageless, as if forcing me to improvise its meaning. And for the first time I realize that I am leaving.

A Summer Dream

Tired, he lay peaceful, open to the warmth and the possibility of sleep. His eyes felt like molten iron as he stared through closed lids at the sun. He felt this but did not see it, think it; he saw instead the cornfields, cows and billboards, which passed by the side of the red-hot ball, faster even now in memory than they had passed all morning. He had carefully watched this roadside mural, while staring over handlebars at a monotonous concrete constant which, before long, became unseen, as the molten mass of his vision became now.

But he felt it as he had felt the road. His whole body was warmed. He could hear the soft, indolent waves lapping, their coolness occasionally paradoxical as one broke hard on the diving raft and sprayed his hot skin. Only then did he feel the light breeze and hear the voices, although he did not look, need to look. They laughed and splashed toward shore, as they no doubt did each day about this time. He did not need to observe this to know it. Being the stranger to this lake, this land, he would be the one to be noticed as something out of place, to be investigated. He listened and heard several voices, two male and one female. It was pleasant to just listen. The diving raft was warm and the ride had been long and was not over yet. The sun is always the same, though, he thought. Although it was really the warmth he was defining.

He had been focusing his attention on the girl's voice and suddenly realized it had disappeared. Then suddenly it returned, close and friendly.

"Hi!"

He turned his head without rising, so that her wet-hair-framed face was sideways, the hot red ball cooling and the sky above and the lake below.

"Hello."

"You're from New York."

"Yes, I am. How'd you know that?"

He wondered if he were in some new, mystical land as he did not think of his bike now, much less the unseen license plate. He just stared at the pretty, sideways face.

"I just know. My name's Lisa."

"I'm John," he said. He did not say "Johnny" as the people who called him that were gone now; maybe he even believed that what he had been was gone too, had gradually disappeared as the gas in the tank between his legs was used up and the old identities grew farther distant and finally were gone. His ship was well over that horizon which we once believed, not so long ago, was the end of the earth and all else beyond an empty void. So maybe I am different now, he even thought as he heard himself speak, realizing he had not really said that much in two days, thinking: or should I say a thousand miles.

"Well, John, from New York, how about giving me a ride on your Harley tonight?"

"Tonight? No, I will be gone by then," he said, not yet thinking, I'm in no hurry; just watching the sideways face which began to seem right, as if sideways or upside down in time makes just as much sense, is just as good a way to see things. He even thought of telling her she was lovely, but he knew he was not that different.

"That can wait," she said, and he knew that she was right. "Wherever you are going can wait for one night. Can't it?"

"I suppose it can."

She smiled, a beautiful, full smile. "Good. Then I will see you tonight at the Wayside. It's up the road a ways. I'll be with Robbie, my brother, the one standing up—." She pointed toward shore and for the first time he looked up and saw them, the two boys—men.

Then, he looked at her. Right-side up she was just as pretty, and it all came together now, as if sideways is fine for beauty, but feeling, love or the possibility of it anyway, could not begin until the beauty agreed with mass and gravity. "—and our friend, Jeff—you can't see him, he likes to swim under water—and I'll know you because of that funny stare of yours and you'll know me 'cause of my big blue eyes and I'll call out your name and you can take me for a ride."

And suddenly she vanished, and in a brief flash he saw her under water: the tanned, quick body broken twice by a blue, two-piece bathing suit, just a bit more than a bikini, and then he did not see her until she surfaced near shore and jumped lightly from the water, waved, and faded into the trees, all at once as if the entire motion had been just a moment, or not really measured in time at all.

As he lay back on the diving raft, he heard her call to the others to come, but they continued laughing and splashing. Then he heard nothing. After a moment, however, he felt that something, someone, had surfaced nearby and was watching him. He turned to look, but it had submerged again. The anonymous eyes had seen him, though. He again listened to laughter come over the water and then, suddenly, it was quiet. After a few minutes he looked. The blue waves lapped against the shore where the birch trees stopped. And that was all. The lake below and the sky above, and she—they —were as if imagined.

HE DOWNSHIFTED AS HE passed the sign that read SHERMAN and below that, Unincorporated, which elicited a vague notion that he should not even stop here. No, what he had seen, the girl, could not have been more than what she was in that moment. *This is what I am leaving, escaping, to prove—that speed and distance will diminish that which otherwise seems to prevail.*

He stopped at the first intersection and automatically planted his foot for support. The town lay before him: Main Street (like others he had seen that day): the grocery; the sporting goods store; the gas stations; the movie theater (this one not closed down, yet); some American flags, and then the end of it just a few blocks away. I should not stop here and find myself in yet another illusory reality; but then: *Maybe I have come the distance needed and it is all right now.*

He pulled into a gas station simply named "Ben's Auto Repair," a Depression-era structure with oil-coated, cracked concrete. He chose it over an antiseptically clean-looking Mobil station that sold bait and food items a block away.

He removed the gas cap and lifted the large, metal handle off the pump. The small tank filled quickly. He returned the handle to the pump and tightened the cap on the tank. A man was working in the station.

"Hello," John said to get his attention. The man looked up reluctantly from an engine he was examining, glanced at the bike and the pump, and wordlessly accepted the money.

John walked back to his motorcycle. He carefully checked each working part. Everything was fine, in good shape. He suddenly realized that he was hungry. There was an orange hamburger stand across the street. He was tired of hamburgers. He started the bike and drove two blocks farther into town, stopping at a rectangular-fronted general store whose sign read Medford's. Some Wisconsin sausage and cheese on a roll would taste good, he thought. He walked into the old store.

Medford's had a hardwood floor, narrow aisles heavily burdened with canned goods, and a section for clothes and souvenirs. It smelled good, like fresh meat and sawdust. John walked to the counter in the back of the store. A balding man wearing thick-lensed glasses was lifting packages off the floor.

"Excuse me," John said. The man looked up. "Could you give me about a quarter pound of that salami and some of that cheese there and maybe just one fresh roll?"

The man took the salami and began slicing.

"You'll have to go 'cross to the bakery for the roll," he said. "All we got are those bags. Half-dozen." He replaced the sausage and took the cheese. "That'll be eighty-five cents."

John reached in his pocket for the change, counted the coins, and gave them to the man. For some reason he felt a need to communicate something more with this stranger.

"This is really a nice town you got here," he said.

The man did not say anything. John noticed that a nearby shopper, a local it seemed, overheard, thinking: *I'll have to ask a question now.*

"Can you tell me how to find the Wayside?"

The man looked up.

"You a troublemaker?"

"Ah, no. I don't think so," he joked to no response. "I'm supposed to meet someone there."

"Well that someone should be locked up and that degenerate hangout should be shut down."

The man looked down at a package he was unwrapping. John began to turn when the man began talking again, looking downward like he was addressing what he was working on, now appearing calm, almost sad.

"I met my wife at the Wayside. Long time ago, when it was a respectable establishment. She's gone now. We had some real good times there. 'Course things were different then—no drugs and all this free sex stuff. It was wholesome, like this country used to be back before it turned into a tourist trap." He paused and then, "Go up the Chain Road, north about a mile."

As the man disappeared into a back room, John took his packages and walked back outside. It was late afternoon, and he would have to wait until dark. The sky was endlessly blue and the air was warm and fresh. The salami would taste good. Then, he would take a nap somewhere—in a pine grove he had noticed near the lake—before going to meet Lisa. She is very lovely, he thought. So fresh and full of unknown secrets like this beautiful country. He crossed the lazy street and took the three steps of the Sherman Bakery in one intoxicated bound.

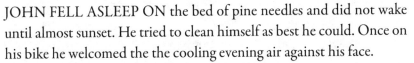

JOHN FELL ASLEEP ON the bed of pine needles and did not wake until almost sunset. He tried to clean himself as best he could. Once on his bike he welcomed the the cooling evening air against his face.

Through a break in the trees he briefly glimpsed an old sign for a place that Humbert Humbert and Lolita most certainly would have stayed that advertised CABINS and below that in hand-painted script the name, The Birches. Perhaps an option for tonight he thought.

A full moon began to rise as he entered the town. A few dressed in their summer Gatsby-esque finest stood outside a nightclub, but that was all the humanity he could find; it took just a few minutes to pass through this locus of civilization. Then, he was again riding between the great stands of timber. Presently, he saw a large, rambling old structure with cars parked in front. He eased through the gears as he drove in the ruts of the parking area. An old sign over the door read, THE WAYSIDE. Two colorful neon beer signs glowed in the windows. He parked near the entrance in a small space between a white, late-model corvette and a rusty Ford pick-up truck.

The building was obviously old, fronted by a spacious porch, which gave slightly under his weight as he opened the door to enter.

Inside, it was crowded and noisy and somewhat smoky. There was a long bar and then a wide opening through which he could see a band setting up, untangling numerous cords apparently with a total lack of confusion. The bell of a pinball machine rang loudly to his right; in a corner to his left two couples were playing an intense game of foosball. He walked over to the bar to get a beer.

Before he could get through the crowd, above the din, he heard a female voice call his name. Lisa, her brother, and the other, he guessed their friend Jeff, sat at a table with a pitcher of beer. Lisa waved for him to come.

He made his way through the crowd mumbling "excuse me" until he stood beside their table. Lisa was radiant. She wore a satin shirt with a denim jacket. Her now-dry brown hair hung lightly on her shoulders. And, she wore bangs, a nuance of style he favored but which had not been popular for quite a few years.

"Would you like to sit down?" Lisa said, returning his stare, unblinking.

He sat down.

"Good. John, I'd like you to meet my brother, Robbie—"

"Hey," John said, holding out his hand, which Robbie shook in the popular "soul" manner of the times. His black hair was almost as long as Lisa's and he sported a bushy beard.

"Pleased to meet you, Johnny," he said, inexplicably calling him by the old identity. "Good to see a new face around this joint."

"As long as they don't move in on his baby sister," Lisa giggled. "And this is our good friend Jeff Tolarski."

"Hi," John said. Jeff looked up from his glass but did not answer or offer his hand.

"Jeff's being rather sullen tonight," Lisa said.

John took a drink from his glass of beer. It tasted good. He drank again and aimed his gaze back at Lisa.

"John's going to give me a ride on his bike," she announced.

"Schwinn?" Jeff said. John looked at him. *So this is how it starts now.*

"What kind of machine you got?" Robbie asked. "Honda, ain't it?"

"It's a Harley, Sportster. Nothing special."

"Well Lisa seems to think so," Jeff said.

"I hear that's a good road bike," Robbie continued.

"Boys, boys," Lisa said. "John here obviously likes to ride and so do I. I'm sure his motorcycle is adequate for providing me with the thrill of a fast and exciting ride tonight."

"Wow what a thrill," Jeff said.

"Oh, Jeff, you're such a bore!" she said. "John, you are going to give me a ride, aren't you?"

"Sure. I'd love to." Jeff was beginning to bother him; he felt the start of that old annoying feeling between two men, caused by one woman. He turned to Robbie. "The Sportster's a good bike for what I'm doing—which is a lot of highway riding."

He finished his beer. Robbie immediately filled it again.

"So how did you enjoy our raft today?" Lisa asked.

"It was very nice. Is it your raft?"

"Sort of. We hang there a lot. Jake's Spring is sort of for everyone."

"Yes, I believe I sensed that when I saw it from the road. Like I had to stop and swim out to the raft. The water was so peaceful. It drew me like a magnet." Thinking of a pamphlet he'd picked up at Medford's he added, "I understand you have quite a few lakes around these parts?"

"We've got mostly water around here, for sure," Robbie answered. "Where did you say you were from?"

"Batavia, New York."

"Where's that?"

"New York."

"Oh."

In a sudden explosion of sound, the band began to play; immediately the voices, the pinball bells, and the laughter took second place to the guitars and drums as they filled the room. John recognized the song by the second chord: Honky Tonk Woman.[1] The local band was on the mediocre side but trying hard; however, he watched Lisa's face light up as the vocals began. *I met a gin-soaked barroom queen in Memphis....* People jumped to the dance floor. Lisa looked at him excitedly.

"C'mon!" she shouted.

"No," he shook his head and also yelled, "I don't dance much."

She looked at him for a second, disappointed. Then, in that mo-

---

1.   https://youtu.be/uMc5znnK-UY

mentary unmotion which John had witnessed at the lake, she was on the floor with Robbie, dancing, spinning, and laughing. John was left with Jeff, who sat quietly and stared at his beer. The pitcher was empty, so John took it to be refilled. The bartender asked which he wanted, Heilmann's or Bud. It must be the first, he thought, I never heard of it back home. He carefully carried the overflowing pitcher of amber fluid back to the table as the band began a Stones medley.

> *Brown Sugar[2]*
> *How come ya dance so good?*
> *Brown Sugar*
> *Just like a young girl should.*

He sat and quickly analyzed the band and then was content to watch Lisa spin and laugh. Bangs, he thought. Of course.

"SO WHERE IS THIS IMPORTANT place you are in such a rush to get to?" Lisa asked.

They were finishing the third pitcher of beer since John arrived. He was beginning to feel it.

"No place in particular. The Canadian Rockies in general."

The band played a current hit with a monotonous melody and a redundant bass line. They had to shout.

"Why?"

"Sorry, why what?"

"Why the Canadian Rockies?"

"I've never seen them."

"Have you seen the Grand Canyon?"

"No. Perhaps I'll get there too."

They looked at each other across the table.

"So what are you leaving?"

Incisive mind this beauty has, too.

"College for one," John began transporting back in time to the old life. "My thesis questioned Fitzgerald's world view regarding man's ability to experience pure love beyond youth, as if the light is temporal and gradually fades and extinguishes." He paused realizing his audience. "But hey, what do I know about F. Scott Fitzgerald?"

"Who?" Lisa shouted to overcome the oppressive music, which was reaching a terrifically inane climax.

"F. Scott Fitzgerald!" He also shouted this to be heard, but the song had abruptly ended first and his words hung in the barroom smoke. Faces turned and looked at him in the moment of silence.

"Never heard of him," Lisa said.

HE WAS STANDING FACING the wall in the men's room. It smelled of the chemicals they put in urinals. Cigarette butts; dadaist art. When the band took their first break, the guitarist had said something to Lisa before going to the bar. *Wonder what? Everyone knows her; but she seems to like me. She's direct, but something in her beauty, a timelessness. Grace.* He remembered her swimming, and the way she dances. I'll have to be careful, though, thinking of her sullen friend. *I know how he feels, but I think I may, could anyway, love her. Why not? Is it impossible? After all, I'm somewhere in the middle of the continent, now.* But the quick thought *Last thing I need is trouble when I'm out of here tomorrow.*

There was a name scrawled on the wall: Debbie. And a phone number. He smiled. Debbie had been his first love. He couldn't quite picture her face. He laughed to himself at everything and depressed the plunger. Whoosh. 555-2637.

About to wash his hands, he could find no soap. He took out his comb and looked in the mirror. His face in the dirty reflection startled him, as if he did not expect to find himself standing there. A stubble of beard was noticeable as he had not shaved in two days. Shaving on the road would be impractical. He decided that he would grow a beard.

As he was about to leave, the door swung open and Jeff entered. They froze, like two animals that are natural enemies.

"Having a good time?" Jeff said.

"Yes. I am, thank you."

"Don't thank me. But let me give you a word of advice." He slurred his words somewhat. "Stay clear of Lisa."

"Is that a threat?"

It was the first time he saw Jeff smile that night.

"No, friend, just advice."

"Well, I'll keep it in mind," he said, opening the door to leave; the noise of the barroom entering the small, smelly room. Jeff grabbed his arm.

"You don't understand."

John shook his arm free and walked out. He was thinking that this surely must be the West.

BACK AT THE TABLE HE thought, *but this isn't the West*. He had been driving north most of the day and began to ponder his exact location.

"How far are we from Lake Superior?" he asked the table in general.

"About 60 miles," Robbie told him. "Straight up the highway."

So all this was happening—he was living it—just stone's throw from Superior's south shore. He could even picture it: the hazy, blue-green hills from which you could see the brief, stony beach and then the powerful gray waves coming immeasurably from the far, misty horizon; under which it is all cold and deep and old. The Natives called it Gitchee Gumee, the French fur traders mapped each bay. The *Edmund Fitzgerald*[3] and many other freighters lay forever preserved in its icy depths due to Superior's furious and unpredictable storms.

What else? Something else. Of course! Along its shores a young boy named Jimmy Gatz spent his time working odd jobs before spotting Dan Cody's yacht bobbing in the awesome waves and, rowing out to meet his new identity and his final destiny, introduced himself to the rich, old man as Jay Gatsby.

He sat alone, surveying the activity. Everyone was busy. Lisa and her brother were dancing. Jeff was talking with someone at another table. The song ended before he noticed what it had been. Lisa came back to the table as the band began an old Beatles hit, the mid-sixties harmonies hitting him like a cold wave breaking on his vision of Dan Cody's yacht.

"Let's dance," he said quick and sure, grabbing Lisa's hand and jumping to the dance floor.

WHEN THEIR DANCE ENDED, John stopped briefly at the board to offer thanks to the sound man, as he had been accustomed to do at the few gigs he had recently played back home.

"Nice mix," he complemented him, a young man about John's age, perhaps a few years older.

"Thanks. These guys aren't too tough, you should see some of the acts that come through here." He added glancing off his levers and offering a hand, "My name's Ed."

"Good to know you Ed. I'm John. Just passing through."

"You in the business?"

"Sort of."

"There's no "sort of" in this business, either you are or you ain't."

John contemplated that thought. Ed was right.

"I am," he responded and turned to re-join his new compatriots, his identity becoming more defined with each stranger he met.

---

3.   *https://youtu.be/rFkyDB2InTs*

"CLIMB ON!" HE YELLED over the roar of the motorcycle. "Swing your leg over and sit close with your arms around me. Put your feet on the pegs."

"I know. I've done this before," she said.

The extra helmet that he always packed just in case made her face even prettier, framed by the hard, white plastic. Steady, now. Then, she was on the bike, tight and soft against his back. He felt her arms close around his jacket as he took off.

The speed was an immediate relief, and the cold blast of night air sobered him quickly. He took the bike up to fifty, then fifty-five, thinking, Is this fast enough for her? Sixty—his hand tightly wrapped around the accelerator grip—

"Slow down!" she yelled in his ear. "Turn left up here." He slowed and made the turn.

They traveled down the Chain Road as through a tunnel, the massive dark walls of the forest surrounded them, edges outlined in blue moon glow. Then the expanse of a lake, its small waves sparkling reflections of the celestial light. John only glanced at it, trying to keep his eyes on the road.

"It's beautiful!" he said over his shoulder, not knowing if she heard. He slowed as they drove over a small bridge. There were lakes to both sides. Then, the woods engulfed them again, the silver road like a magic pathway through the darkness.

"Go slow," he heard distinctly over the purring of the engine, as if the words were also etched in the night. "There'll be a dirt road on the right."

He followed her instructions and turned into the narrow, sandy drive, proceeding with just enough momentum to keep the bike from tipping. Suddenly there was a clearing in the forest; a log cabin stood in the shadows. Beyond he saw a large, silvery lake. He brought the bike to a stop near a garage shed.

"Shut it off," she yelled.

She jumped off, her hair flying as she removed the helmet. He also disembarked, and they stood drenched in a milky glow, standing on luminous sand.

"It's so quiet," he whispered. "This your uncle's place?"

She nodded. "He doesn't use it much anymore. Was here more when my aunt was alive." She looked toward the lake as if she had just noticed it. "Come here."

She took his hand and led him down to the lake. He followed her onto a wood pier, its old planks answering each careful step they made. The end made a T, on which rested a bench. Its finish was worn considerably by the winds of many long, icy winters it had withstood, bravely facing Laurie Lake.

They sat down on the bench. He could not help staring at the wonderfully desolate scene stretched out before him, so large that the individual waves finally became a single shimmering whole like a liquid moon, above which, far away—over a mile, he guessed—was the thin, dark line of the opposite shore. The sky above them was the entire Milky Way; an occasional shooting star appeared and died as it fell.

"I have never seen anything like this; anything that really felt just like this," he said and shivered, turning to face her eyes.

She smiled and he felt like he would melt in the cold moonlight.

"Are you in love?" she asked abruptly.

He sat frozen not sure of a response.

"I mean with a girl back in New York. I don't think this is just because of, what's his name, F. Scott?"

"Oh," he said, somewhat relieved, but her perceptive eyes were on him. "That was partly true. There was a girl—"

"I knew it."

"No—that's all over. I suppose I may have been in love with her. Just wasn't what she was looking for in the end."

"That sounds like an old movie."

"Maybe it does," he said defensively.

She looked at him.

"So what do you do when you're not at school, which I guess you're not anymore?"

"I'm a songwriter. Should say wannabe."

Her gaze narrowed. "Really? Will you write a song about me?"

"Perhaps. You never know. It's dangerous to be a friend of a writer."

"I like danger," she paused. "Where's your guitar?"

"Long story."

She looked around the limitless lake and landscape.

"We've got time."

"Was running out of gas money downstate and thought I'd do some busking. Evidently they've got a local ordinance against that sort of thing. Sheriff threw me in the local tank."

"What?" she exclaimed.

"Yeah. And took my guitar. They let me go after I agreed to do a few hours of community service—which is what I thought I was doing—I asked him for my guitar back. He just said, 'That's now the property of the state. Now it's time for you to get out of my town boy.' " He laughed, "It was my road guitar, no big deal, I'll replace it down the line."

"Well I hope to hear you on the radio someday."

"That's unlikely. My singing is worse than my playing. I mostly write."

"So what about Nashville?"

"Thought's crossed my mind. Perhaps on the road home, wherever home is these days. I've heard some exciting stuff coming out of there lately, not the same old heavy-on-the-strings stuff. There's this new guy named Kristofferson. Also Texas, writer down there who knocks me out, name of Townes Van Zandt."

"Funny names. Never heard of them."

"Not surprising. But I think you may down the line."

"I don't know much about country music."

"Do you like those new Stones songs?"

"Of course, Jumpin' Jack Flash is indeed a gas."

"Well, those tunes come straight out of Bakersfield country and a guy Keith Richards knew name of Gram Parsons. He was bringing it all together. Pity he died a couple years ago."

They sat bathed in the moonlight, both considering all the possible futures this new information imagined.

He glanced at her, considering. "I do have a new song I've been working on that might turn into something, maybe it could be about you. Working title "Remember the Words.""

"Oh please let me hear it. Please please!"

"Like I told you, no guitar, and only a couple verses so far."

"Well just give me a sample. Acapulco.

"A capela."

"Yeah like that."

He cleared his throat and began,

As the sun slowly slides by the willow
And sets in a sky oh so red
I see how the willow is weeping
And remember the words that you said.

"Sounds sad," Lisa said after a moment. "Do I make you sad?"

"We'll see," he said without thinking except about the lyrics. "I need a second verse, but I think the third goes like this."

I could pack all my things and just drive off
To a place your thoughts haven't touched.
But when I get there I'd find all of nothing
'Cause I wouldn't be leaving with much,
No I wouldn't be leaving with much.

"OK, that's obviously about that girl back home. But I think I like it so far, your voice is really nice," she offered. "I hope I'm not part of that 'all of nothing' line."

They sat quiet watching the shimmering waves become one with the moon.

She leaned forward and kissed him lightly on the lips. His head reeled, and he felt like he might fall into the lake.

He moved close to her and took her in his arms. He stroked her hair as he had wished to all evening, and bunched it together in his fist, soft and warm. She smelled fresh and wholesome. Her soft mouth sought his completely; her breath becoming quick.

"I know where there's a hidden key," she whispered.

"What?"

"A key. For the cabin. I know where my uncle hides it."

He looked at her, understanding. It bothered him that he had not thought it before. But I love her, he thought. I love her so.

"Do you think your uncle—" he began.

She laughed. "He never comes here anymore since Aunt Millie died. He just stays in town, working all day in the back of our store—"

"Medford's?" he exclaimed involuntarily. "Yes, I believe I met him today. Told me he met his wife at the Wayside. Said it should be closed down now—"

"That's him."

"He's your uncle?"

"Yep. Uncle Bob. My dad owns the store. I'm Lisa Medford."

He kissed her to seal this belated introduction, but then he stood. He felt dizzy. An image came to mind of the guitarist saying something to her as the band ended the set. He began to walk toward shore.

"Come on, Lisa Medford."

She followed him.

"What's wrong?" she said.

"Nothing," he said. "I don't know."

He turned then to see her against the lake, as if he might never again see anything as beautiful. He almost said "Get the key" but instead he walked toward the motorcycle.

"Let's go back now," he said.

"But—"

"Let's just finish our ride now."

She shrugged and climbed on the bike as he jumped on the starter. The engine roared as they followed the dirt lane back again, leaving the moonlit cabin standing as solitary as they had found it, its secrets fortified behind the steel padlock and the sturdy popple logs.

AS THEY PULLED INTO the Wayside parking lot, a group was assembled by the entrance. Lisa pointed to a pickup toward the back, and he was already stopping next to it when he noticed Jeff and Robbie sitting on its opened end.

When the engine died, someone in the group, a man's voice, shouted, "Hey Lisa! Moonlight skinny dip at Otterbein's!"

"Later!" she yelled. John could not tell who had called to her, although several faces watched them.

"Keith Otterbein's parents are millionaires," she informed him, as if that explained everything.

Robbie greeted them. "Have a nice ride?"

"Very nice," Lisa said. "We went out to Uncle Bob's and back. His bike is so fast."

"It's a boy toy," Jeff exhaled, passing something to Robbie as John realized what they were doing. Robbie held it out.

"Hit?"

He was about to decline when Lisa took it and sucked steadily, holding it in for about thirty seconds before exhaling.

"I'd like to see you drive that 'toy,' " she exhaled with each word in a sarcastic, challenging tone that seemed quite natural; holding the joint between two fingers for John to take. It would be foolish to refuse, he thought.

"As a matter of fact, Jeffrey was just telling me that he is skilled in the operation of such a vehicle," Robbie said. Lisa coughed out the smoke in a burst of laughter.

"Piece . . . of . . . cake," Jeff said, inhaling with each word.

"C'mon, Jeff. You have trouble shifting gears in the truck!" Lisa said, and Robbie joined her in laughter.

Jeff stood with his eyes downcast, defenseless, and, as John watched, seemed to proffer a more sympathetic appearance—as if he was revealing the person he was when the girl was not there, when he did not have to act this role in a silly, though probably universal, melodrama. John was beginning to comprehend the intense feelings this strange girl (whom others accepted with an apparent indifference of common, though beautiful, property) stirred in Jeff and himself. Where he had felt the stirrings of jealous animosity, he now began to feel something commiserative, which became an almost empathetic sense of despair.

"Want to take her for a ride?" John asked, the words in the air before he even thought them. He held out the keys.

"I don't have to prove anything," Jeff said.

"Oh, but I think you do," Lisa challenged. "You keep all these talents so well hidden."

Jeff grabbed the keys from John and walked to the motorcycle. *I hope he knows what he's doing, I've got to leave here tomorrow.*

"Just go up to the bend and come back," John instructed as Jeff kicked the starter and the bike roared.

Jeff moved the bike slowly toward to the road. *He seems to know what he's doing. Good, now shift; shift now... No!"*

Jeff, in attempting to shift, ran off the road, lost control on the shoulder, and wiped out. He seemed not to be hurt and stood up. Then, he began to lift the heavy machine off the ground.

"No!" John yelled. "Leave it! Don't—"

But too late. He had managed to lift it, but could not hold it up. It crashed on the other side while Jeff stood helpless.

"You idiot!" Lisa hissed as the four now stared at the fallen motorcycle.

John quickly checked the damage. Fluid trickled into the gravel beside the road: the oil case was cracked. And the left directional light was smashed. He could find no other serious damage, however.

"I'm sorry." Jeff removed the helmet. "I couldn't find second and lost control."

"No kidding," Lisa said.

"Real good, Jeffrey. What else do you do?" Robbie laughed.

"I'm sorry," he repeated. "I'll pay for its repair."

"That's all right," John said. He was as amazed to find his heart go out to Jeff as he was to find Lisa and Robbie laughing at their friend. His motorcycle bleeding and sprawled at an angle to the road, he felt as if he should apologize to it for destroying its neutrality by involving it with these people. He looked up at Lisa.

"I think I can fix it in town."

"Well, the least we can do is put you up for the night," Robbie offered, looking at Lisa. "Our little brother's over at a friend's so you can use his bed."

"Mom didn't let him go," Lisa said.

"Oh. Well, no problem," he laughed. "John can sleep in your bed."

John felt nauseated and looked to the night sky to avoid getting sick. He noticed an open field on a ridge across the road.

"I'll sleep over there," he said. "It won't rain tonight."

HE MOVED THE MOTORCYCLE across the road and hid it in some small evergreens. He took his sleeping bag and climbed the hill, up toward a ridge where the wild grass pierced the heavens in millions of bright pin-holes. He thought—perhaps half believing—that if you went far enough, past even the illusion of the black void, the universe would be one pure, bright luminous Being everywhere at the same time.

He spread out the sleeping bag and lay on the cool earth, trying to get the full moon to stay fixed in one place in the sky while he tried to organize his exploding thoughts. He remembered reading somewhere that one should never sleep in the moonlight—that scientists had proof it causes madness. He studied the moon carefully, its blemishes and craters, and then thought of the television picture he had watched so intently just a few years earlier in July 1969: the silver, bubble-headed men walking around up there. Were they actually walking on that globe of light in the heavens? *Its not really that far....*

Something moved to his right. He quickly turned his head to see. Lisa stood a dozen feet away, covered with the ghostly glow. She did not say anything. She had brushed back her bangs, he noticed, as he wondered how long she had been watching.

"Hello, again," he said. It was stupid not to talk. She did not answer. "I thought you were going to the party at that rich kid's."

"I didn't feel like it," she said, taking one small, awkward step forward.

"Why not?"

"Look, I think you got the wrong idea. About me, whatever. I've watched your apparent interest in me go from intense desire to like I might as well not exist. Are the girls in New York that much nicer?"

"No."

"Then on what scale are you judging me?"

"On an imaginary one, I suppose."

"Well, I'm not just a character in one of your songs. I'm quite real."

She came and sat down in the tall grass beside his sleeping bag.

"I suppose you are," he said.

"I don't belong here."

"Where?"

"Here. In Sherman."

"Where do you belong?"

"I don't know. California maybe. I'll be leaving soon as I save enough money."

He didn't know what she was saying and didn't really care. Once again he just stared sideways at the pretty face.

"Why do you treat Jeff like that?" he asked.

"Jeff? He's, well, just Jeff."

"He's in love with you."

She sighed. "I know. Isn't that silly? We've grown up together. He's such a fool."

"You don't believe in love?"

"Sure, but—. Hey, next thing you'll be telling me I should settle down with him. On a farm maybe? Have a bunch of kids?"

"No," he paused. "You can't understand that?"

"Well—. Oh, come on! You must realize it's the seventies?"

"Yes. I realize it."

"Of course you do. So why are we talking about Jeffrey?"

"Sometimes when I talk about someone else I begin to understand myself."

"Well, you're not like Jeff. You're from back East for one thing."

"That makes me different?"

"It makes you better. The way I see it—I've thought about this—this country's got sort of a big crack running straight down the middle, and all the burning, liquid rock comes out there and flows to the coasts. We are hot and shapeless here, and we gradually become real as we reach the oceans—and then we're all solid and definite and, and... stoned!" She laughed. "That was pretty decent grass, hey?"

"Yeah, I'm still...."

"Jeff doesn't flow like the rest of us. He's molten rock that's caught in an eddy—doomed to be forever...."

John lay pondering this crazy girl's thoughts. He vaguely knew that she had stood and was moving somehow, but he did not look. Instead, he said:

"You asked me why I left home. It wasn't just the girl, and it wasn't just college. I think what happened is I looked around and I was drawn into the unknown—"

Then he looked at her. She had slipped out of her jacket and shirt and stood half naked, looking very much like a marble statue in the blue moonlight: *Aphrodite, he thought, after the Greek Praxiteles. Why is she so beautiful so lovely so perfect when I know that she is not?*

"Can I come in now?" she asked.

"What the hell," he said opening the flap of his sleeping bag.

THE MORNING WAS CLEAR and bright and had the feeling of heartbreak. This is a northern morning, he thought, as he walked the motorcycle the half mile or so into town.

After a visit to the garage he'd stopped on his way into town, with some help from a worker who was in very early, he knelt beside the curb, completing repairs on the oil case, when he felt someone standing behind him on the sidewalk.

"Is it OK?" Lisa asked.

"Oh yeah, nothing serious."

"Are you leaving already?"

She had left him sometime during the night. Now, he turned to look, but she stood so that the low sun was precisely behind her head, the sun rays shone from the burning edges of golden hair. It was an eclipse, the brightness of the aura hid her face.

"Yep. I was lucky enough to find everything I needed in this little town of yours. So just a few more adjustments here—"

"Why don't you stay a few days? You can stay with us."

He looked at the eclipse (didn't they say never look directly at it?).

It was easy not seeing the face.

"No. Thanks. I truly appreciate it but I gotta be moving on."

He felt her quiet presence as he worked fixing the directional. He had wished that he would not see her today.

"Can I come with you?"

Somehow he expected the words, the request, maybe in the moment he had first seen her at the lake, as if she carried it on her lips until this time when he could answer.

"No, I'm afraid not. We are not going the same way."

Then he would feel her move away. There would be the one moment of movement, he knew, when he could turn his head and see her, having moved past the eclipse and before she disappeared, all at once like before but still within his power to stop; even to undo or re-wind the events and change them, alter the outcome he had himself willed into motion. But he allowed that moment to pass. He felt a certain draining emptiness as he looked up and saw a deserted Main Street: the rectangular-fronted stores, the American flags, a tourist looking into the fish display box; but he thought, maybe that's it: the motion of your own ideals willed into their inevitable though unknown outcomes; the irrevocable and ponderous and maybe even laughable decisions which are singularly yours to bear, which are the only means you have to deflect, or maybe, if you can believe it, even to help direct the haphazard and unthinking path fate draws for your life, which, to fate, is just another leaf in the autumn air. No one else really knows because they cannot see the lines you draw, the roads you take. You are alone to determine the world; there is no audience to laugh or cry. There is just you, and the man at the fish box two empty sun-filled blocks away.

And the machine, he thought as he left the town behind, traveling north past the lakes, the Wayside, the Sherman Outdoor. This machine will take me there almost before my slow-moving will can determine the course. Just as the railroads reached the West; as Apollo placed men gently on the moon. It must be important, he thought, to will the machine properly. Otherwise we will find ourselves flying into a future that is unworthy of our past.

He saw the hitch-hiker a long way down the road. It occurred to him that he should stop, maybe just to see if a stranger at this time could change these thoughts—who might say, "No, you got it all wrong. This is how it is."

He pulled onto the shoulder and approached the figure who had turned and was walking, dressed in denim, a knapsack over his back. John revved the engine and the hitch-hiker turned.

It was Jeff.

"I see you got your bike fixed," he shouted.

John shut off the engine.

"It wasn't that bad. Fixed it in a couple hours. Where are you heading?"

"I don't know. I just found myself on this side of the road."

"Why?" John asked.

"I guess she laughed at me once too often. " He paused. "I'm sorry about the way I acted last night. I wasn't in control of things."

"I know. Neither was I," John said, considering this stranger anew.

John looked down the road. Then he turned and unfastened the spare helmet. It was more a gesture than an invitation.

"Here, put it on. Hop on the back of ol' Rocinante here. "We'll head up toward Lake Superior. Then we'll stop in Duluth for some burgers. You can decide then where you want to go."

Jeff took the helmet and mounted the motorcycle. John kicked the starter, and they accelerated along Highway X. John's thoughts rushed with the speed: It is cumulative, over space and time. It does add up. Only the second day gone and I meet and fall half in love with strangers I never met before and whom I'll no doubt never see again, who have nevertheless joined me in something—eternal. *I'll have plenty of time to think about it, though.*

He watched as the beautiful, seemingly endless forest flowed by and smelled the piney-fresh rush of air while his thoughts disintegrated with the rhythm of the engine and the tar-stripped road, the evenly spaced lines keeping the beat as a song played in his head.

One hundred years from this day[4]
Will the people still feel this way
Still say the things that they're saying right now?
Everyone said I'd hurt you,
They said that I'd desert you
If I go away
You know I'm gonna get back somehow...

---

4.   *https://youtu.be/pvR9EHWdOAc*

The Guitar

W*hat's my offense officer?*
    Disturbing the peace.
Well thanks for the review, but I was just busking for the locals.
I don't care if you were husking corn, you don't have a permit to make noise with that thing on our public streets.
How long am I going to be in here?
Until we can get ol' Judge Johnson to schedule a hearing.
This is ridiculous, I was just passing through town.
Yeah nice Harley, it's waiting for you in the pound.
A pause and then the captor's voice became a bit softer, with a tone that brought to Raymond's mind the man with the meek face and glasses.
Tell you what, Johnny boy is it? I'll just take that geetar of yours as your fine and we'll call it a day. Oh and we'll throw in a couple hours of community service so I can tell the chief we struck a deal. Pick up trash around the park.
My guitar? A short laugh. What, you play?
Hell no. I just see it's the only thing of value to you.
A long pause.
Shit. You da man right? If it's the only way out of this.
The heavy lock echoed open and the soundless transaction took place.
Next time schedule an event down at the Legion. You ain't half bad.
Thanks a lot.
And the shuffling of feet away out of range of hearing.

RAYMOND LAY FACING the bleak, gray wall, pretending it was as the old wooden wall had once been when he was younger and his mind was calm though curious. Sometimes he found he could take his mind back to that time, but it had to be falling asleep, when he would close his eyes and remember until the present faded. He tried this sometimes during the day, but it was best at night. It was a trick he learned. Or rather it just happened, as everything just happens. His mind could not be confined to his entrapped body; where his thoughts wandered is where he also traveled.

Of course, ten years alone in small, barren rooms is long enough for things like that to happen. The where of escape was easy. He just closed his eyes. But the endless, recurring images did not cease, such as the image of the meek face with glasses and a mole on the left cheek, along the jawline. It still came back to wake him with pounding heart and wet bedclothes. Nothing ever happened to change that. And, of course, there was no more escaping it than there was escaping his physical confinement.

For many years the images morphed into questions, such as: Why had he done it? The questions were on occasion followed by what passed for answers that attempted to become words which he tried to write down in a little notebook.

ONE DAY (THOUGH THE idea of time had become meaningless) a prison worker, not a guard, rolled a cart of items past Raymond's cell. The overburdened cart contained various items that had been removed from other inmates for whatever reason, usually punitive, and the guitar the busker had used to purchase his freedom was on it. Raymond asked if he could have the guitar. The man with the cart looked at Raymond, who had never caused him any trouble, and without interest or judgment tossed the guitar into Raymond's hands.

"Don't know what you're going to do with it in here but the guards

better not hear it," the man with the cart said.

The guitar sat mutely in the corner of his cell. It remained there for days and weeks and months. Raymond would not touch it for fear it would be taken away. It had become a thing of beauty to him. He sat and stared at its fine curves and taut strings and its fat, hollow body that would resonate wonderfully... if only.

Raymond had trouble remembering the times when his father would play the guitar. He recalled religious songs such as Family Bible[1] that his father would earnestly sing. But there was too much interference for a clear memory of those times. He did not like to think about his father and what had happened. But now and then, staring at the guitar, certain images appeared of the older man teaching Raymond how to play a few songs. The images did not last long in his head.

He wondered how he would play if anything from that other life would return. Soon, it seemed to him that he knew precisely where his fingers would go on the fret board in order for the melody to come alive in his now ever more interior space.

The questions still haunted him in the dark. But soon the words began to fade, no longer pounding soundlessly in his head. What replaced them was difficult for Raymond to understand, for it seemed that the words and images that had echoed within his quiet though turbulent mind had become notes, which began to come together as melodies. Some were very beautiful and some were quite ugly. Soon the melodies began to replace the unknowns, not as answers to the questions, but as something that began to fill that empty space in his head that had forever, it seemed, sought a degree of finality, of peace.

When he looked in the notebook at the crude attempts at the truths he had written, they seemed silly. He had since stopped writing words in the little book. He read, "She loved me and she loved him too. So what is wrong with that? Shouldn't all men love as much as they can," and it seemed ridiculous to him. *I'm not much of a writer*, he

---

1.   https://youtu.be/vMfr6Yb04E4

thought. He sat and gazed at the guitar thinking, *The only answers are the ones I could play on that. I know how they would sound. They would tell me.*

One night he was lying on his bunk facing the gray wall, unable to sleep. A distorted image of the meek face filled his mind. It changed shape, fluid. He could not lose it. Soon, discordant yet somehow structured music replaced the face, becoming the face. It was loud and then soft and the melodies intertwined. As Raymond tossed and turned he seemed to understand their forms. He pictured the guitar and it all seemed to come together. He knew how to create it. His fingers would move in the proper manner and it would exist for the instant of the playing and he could free it for good.

Now he was sitting, his mind carefully arranging the music that came in major and minor chords. But it came so fast and was getting away before he could properly free it. It sounded and faded and echoed in all his being.

He got up and moved to the corner of his cell. He slowly picked up the instrument and went back to the bunk and sat down. His hands began to work out the melody a little at a time as he felt it and as he saw it. He was filled with a joy unlike any he could remember. It was not even difficult. It was becoming free and he could hear it with his own ears, made free by his own hands. For that moment at least, it seemed, for once, there were no questions. He tried something more complicated, and the music waited patiently for him.

"Well, Raymond, old boy, you done become a real musician."

Raymond looked at the guard, then down at the guitar in his hands, fully aware for the first time of its—of his—external existence. It was useless now. He saw the man's pale and sarcastic face. The guard took the guitar and smashed it against the gray stone wall. The music played loud in Raymond's mind. The guitar was smashed again and was in pieces when the guard smashed it once more.

Raymond's hands were now on the man's thin neck. He pressed and pressed. The guard choked and gasped, and it became part of the now hideous crescendo. His hands continued until the man lay limp and it became very quiet in the prison.

He was sitting in the funny, hard chair that had wires attached. And just as the switch clicked and the electricity flowed free, Raymond's mind sounded one final, perfect minor chord of ultimate relief.

The Cutover

A*nd so we remember Thomas Fine....*

THOMAS COMPLETES THE circle of men by sitting on a low stump on which also rests his crosscut saw.

"Mind your arse," Franz Kohler says. " 'Less that's how you play your Swedish fiddle!" The men laugh. Thomas brings the cold fork to his mouth and begins to chew the beans. They are hard and glue-like. He eats quickly, before they freeze on his plate.

It is still cold, but it feels like spring after the past four months in the barren woods. A heavy fog surrounds the circle, and the world consists of only these men and their words. It is March, and they have clear-cut almost every tree in the pinery. The men will be paid in five days and they will then spend it in another five days on drinking and whoring. Then will come the work of rolling logs or working at the mill waiting for next November and the next logging town.

Shawn McBride has finished eating and has placed a generous pinch of snoose in his cheek. "Leave the lad be. He's a hard worker." He laughs hoarsely. "He's earned his promotion from the camp's chick-adee!"

"Ah!" Franz says. "Leave the frozen horse dung be! Thomas Fine is a jack from head to frozen toes."

Thomas smiles wryly. "May a deadly widowmaker cross your path."

"If that be my fate, let it wait till after payday! I've been five months on credit and womenless; just five more days to pay off the wanigan,

then—look out Sherman!"

There is a moment of silence at the mention of money and women. Visible puffs of breath replace words. During the short lunch break they are usually silent—almost reverent with their weary thoughts. But today the joking has begun and will not stop now with thoughts of pay-day.

They all look at Shawn. Franz voices the common thought: "Won't you be heading down to Elksburg like last spring, Shawn?"

Shawn spits out a piece of the snoose. "No, Franz. We busted up that burg last year, but two years in a row is bad luck. 'Sides," he lowers his voice and each man leans forward, "I saw the train arrive at Sherman Station Sunday. Know what it brought?"

"Yes?" they hiss.

"The most beautiful wenches I've seen since I left Nova Scotia."

Thomas has been ignoring his fellow woodsmen, but now looks up.

"They have just arrived from the Chippewa stands—solely for our pleasure. They're already setting up at the hotel on the edge o' town back o' the station."

Billy Bedeaux explodes with a cat call, but for the most part the men are quiet with the news, their heavy labor not quite finished. Soon the boss calls them back to work from somewhere beyond an opaque wall of fog. As they move from the camp in the clear-cut back into the remaining woods, Shawn continues: "There was one red-head the likes of which made me homesick for me land o' heather. I shall have her in my muzzle-loader!"

They laugh and carry their saws deep into the fog. Thomas also fades into the fog, but, unnoticed, he walks off in a different direction, down the rutted road toward camp and town.

THE DOOR OPENS AND he smells it, remembering.

"I'd like to see Audrey, please."

The fat madam laughs, a snort.

"Ain't you about four days early, sonny?"

"Are you open for business yet?"

" 'Course. What, you jacks think you're the only—"

"Well, I'd like to see Audrey then."

"—there's a few husbands around town too, ya know?" She looked at him anew with suspicion. How do you know her name anyway?"

Thomas does not answer.

"All right. You'll be the first customer in... what town is this? Never mind. That'll be two eagles."

"I just want to talk with her."

"You deaf and daft too?"

"I don't get paid until the weekend. Could you credit me?"

The madam laughs scornfully.

"We'll see you Saturday, jack."

"All right. Could you please tell her, then, to meet me at the cafe? In the hotel?"

"You really think one of my girls is going to cross those tracks and walk down that street in broad daylight and force them townsfolk to face their own hypocrisy? You are a young jack."

"Please, I'm begging you. Tell her I'll be waiting here." He looks around. "Over there," he points to stairs on the side of the building.

The madam stares at the strange figure whose words are foreign to her. "Sure, I'll tell her. But you may have a long wait. Audrey isn't the type to go see a jack and not get paid for it."

He stands next to the wood-planked stairway. The wood is rough and white—freshly cut. He sits and waits an hour. Then he hears the board steps move before hearing the voice.

"Stand up, jack, and tell me what you want—why you asked for me. Be it known, I have a pistol in this here wrap."

He turns to face her. She stands on the landing, a wool shawl covers her faded cotton dress. *It was worth it; the suffering is over now.*

"It's me, Audrey. Me—Thomas Fine."

"What do you want, jack?"

"Last year. Elksburg—the Powder Ridge stands. Don't you remember?"

"What do you want?"

"I want to marry you, Audrey."

"You have been out in them woods too long. Goodbye, jack." She turns to leave.

"Wait!" He begins to climb the stairs after her as she whirls around.

"Not another step. I'll put a bullet through your crazy head."

"Listen to me, Audrey. Please! Do you want to do this?"

"Oh, I'm just having a ball, honey."

"Then why?"

"Why do you go out into those wretched woods in November and freeze your arse off until May for enough money to blow it all in one week on corn mash and women like me? You're the reason I'm here, jack."

"My name's Thomas. You know. Thomas Fine. And that's just it. But you see, you and I can break with it now. We can be free. I will be paid this Friday—"

"Well I hope you have a good time."

He had practiced what he'd say but it's not being spoken—

Listen. What you have done—just think what you have done to your body, to your self, more than just the physical selling of the flesh. Do you know what a cutover is? It is what we have done to this magnificent forest around here. We have stripped the land of everything that it had; there's no more than stumps and burnings and frozen mud where once, before we arrived, was a wonderful proud and inviolate woodland. Now it's a cutover. Don't you see? That is what you have done to your body and soul—what we have done to you, for what else could we make of love after ravaging the land. We ravage you.

She turns to go back inside.

He bounds up the stairs and grabs her by the arms and immediately feels how frail she is compared with everything he has held all winter. She faces him, scared, and he feels the hard press of the pistol barrel in his abdomen. As he wonders if she will pull the trigger, anticipating the unknown feeling to shoot through his insides as he falls down the stairs, a train pulls into Sherman Station. They are no more than fifty feet from the rails. There is a horrific tearing screech of locked wheels against frozen tracks. She looks up from him at the train as it sits—motionless, heavy, throbbing steel; then its doors open, flooding the platform with a herd of men.

"Customers," she hisses.

He shakes her, hoping to feel some weighted resistance. He regains his thoughts.

"Don't you see what you and I have to do now? Isn't it terribly obvious? We are guilty of the same sin. We can't walk away from it. I accept the responsibility for the devastation, but now I must farm it, heal it; through the same labor of the body which caused the destruction, I must now plant the seeds to save it. And you must help. You must repudiate what you have done to the landscape of your own soul. Become my wife and allow me to plant my seed in your body, to again bring fertility to your womb and wholeness to your soul."

She looks from the train to him in numbed though pained comprehension, becoming mesmerized by his crazy words and the way they somehow make sense outlined in the cold air by the sound of the train's hissing and the hollow pounding of cargo on the platform.

"I am cold now and want to go in," she says. He releases her. "I have a job to do this weekend, and it is not a happy one. It is, however, my lot in life."

She opens to door to enter, scared and will-less, unbelieving though touched.

"Come to see me when it's over," she says and closes the unpainted door behind her.

THOMAS FINE LOOKS AROUND the small building. The man sits beside a wood stove. There are several boats resting upside down on wooden horses, their smooth, swollen hulls look like a herd of playful whales.

"I'd like to fish."

The man lifts the large axe. "Just break yourself a hole and drop your line."

"How much?"

"Ach, just bring it back when you're done. There's a bench out back if you want to use it. Say, you're a shanty lad. Why aren't you down at J.P.'s?"

He smiles faintly, "Can't catch any fish there. Thank you very much—"

"Hold on! You'll need some of these."

Thomas takes the minnows and the rest of his provisions and awkwardly makes his way out the door, from the woodburning warmth into the more familiar cold of the northern spring.

The axe breaks the ice with an almost thankful ease after the long, dead winter, and the icy water accepts his baited hook. He sits on the bench and puts the end of the pole under his leg. He draws the coat around his body and turns the collar up. He feels good and thinks: *It is good to fish through the ice, to catch your own food with a season's pay still in your pocket.*

There is much noise and commotion from town, a few hundred yards away. His winter friends have been drinking and whoring and fighting for going on twelve hours. He is calmly undisturbed looking out over the barren stretch of snow, which no longer ends with the monumental pines of the shoreline. They are gone now, right down to the lake's edge. In a few weeks the snow will melt and the water will run down to the lakes, muddy, gullied, full of the precious topsoil created over so many calm centuries. The water will no longer be clear and fresh. They have not spared one tree. His friends drink and whore. He sits, the money in his pocket, safe.

His cold hands wrapped tightly around the cane pole, he feels tired. His eyes won't stay open, and his head falls into the warm fur collar. Now he is dreaming, transported into a different scene. Here it is green, lush green with damp mosses, wet trees, and lichen. The moss smells sweet and musky. The place is old; there are tombstones all around him. They rise above his body as he lies cold and damp among them. His head cannot move, he is dead. There are children coming to play all around the moss-covered graves and trees. He cannot speak or open his eyes. Somehow, he watches the children play.

Suddenly he realizes someone lies beside him. Another head rests on the same slab of stone. It is Audrey. She is also dead. He cannot turn his head; he wants to hold her—to take her in his arms, but he cannot move. Lightning flashes through the green. She is no more than six inches away.

His numb hands move and he clutches with unknowing urgency at the sudden life that pulls him from his dream. The green memory is relinquished slowly as he sees himself holding a long cane pole which is twitching madly.

The pole almost jumps from his numb hands. He tries to tighten his grip without feeling and it seems to work. The taut line dances across the small dark hole, bouncing from side to side of the ice. Sensation begins to return, and he feels the strength, the huge force of life that he fights. Its head breaks water, its gaping, outraged jaws try to throw the puny hook. He pulls sharply, and the fish flies from the black hole onto the ice. The large northern pike jumps madly, refusing the foreign atmosphere. It is almost a yard long.

He picks up the large ax, which feels light in his muscled hands as the fish did not. He lifts carefully, aiming, and brings the blunt end down on the fish's head.

It will be a good meal, he thinks as he walks back toward the streets of town. He has been left with just the fragrance of his dream and he shivers. The sun has just set. The fresh fish will taste wonderful. His hand moves into his pocket as he feels the the bundle of paper money. *Tomorrow I will go talk with the man about buying the land.*

He walks slowly, carrying the dead fish, down the rutted road into the blue world of not yet spring.

"THOMAS! WAKE UP! THOMAS!"

He stirs, unwilling to wake.

"Thomas, wake up. They killed Billy!"

"Franz—what did you say?"

"Billy's dead. Down at J.P.'s. Couple hours ago. Merchant in town crushed his head with a fresh-cut two-by-four."

"Why? What did Billy do?" As Thomas becomes fully awake, he sees that Franz is far from sober.

"Insulted his wife, or so the shopkeeper claims. She was walking by the saloon and, you know Billy, he's been so looking forward to the women—"

"Didn't anyone bother to show him the way to the doll house?" Thomas asks, watching the puffs of his breath as if he could see the incredible words he hears himself utter.

"Sure, we all been there, but you know Billy. Those ladies were just so nice too. Say, where were you anyway? You know, you might not get another crack at them, and I mean they were worth every—"

"What do you mean?" Thomas demands, warming himself with growing anger. "What do you mean I might not get another chance?"

"Well maybe if you hurry in right now. But it is Sunday morning, and judging from what I heard—"

"What did you hear?" Thomas thunders.

"That the womenfolk in town are going to march down to that doll house and tear the place apart with stones and clubs. Their men folk will smile and watch no doubt—to see their wives do that for them. 'Sides, they all been there."

Thomas has jumped from the bunk and is frantically trying to get his boots on. His thoughts explode... the order has been lost again... how can they?... they don't understand.

"No," he says. "They can't."

"Look, if you—"

"What time is it, Franz?"

"It's somewhere around nine, I guess."

"Was there... did you see a red-haired girl?"

"Where? Oh, the whore—"

"Shut up!" Thomas roars. "Enough!" He leaps from the ill-constructed log dwelling as Franz Kohler watches, thinking, trying to think, the long chaotic day and night still senseless in his dull mind. Then, finally, he sees.

"No," Franz whispers. "No."

"COME IN. IT'S NOT LOCKED."

"Hello, Mr. Kohler."

"Mr. Kohler? Why the formality, Bob? Come here and sit by the fireplace with me. I'm trying, futilely it seems, to thaw my old bones. It was a nice funeral, wasn't it?"

"Yes, I'm sure Thomas would have approved. Franz, is there anything you would like me to say, you know, in the paper, about Thomas Fine?"

"You mean as the last of a dying breed? No, I understand. Tom and I have been friends for a long, long time. I was just thinking of the old days."

"The lumbering days?"

"Yes. When we were young lumberjacks. You know, its hard to remember everything at will. But today my memory became clear. It's as if Tom's death was a sign for me to remember, to think about what I, we, did, what happened almost a century ago. I'm old and cautious now so it scares me to remember so well."

"You mean that time you and Thomas first camped here? You told me about that when I first came to Sherman. You told me the whole story, about how Thomas fell for that prostitute, and that the townspeople tore apart the whorehouse and beat up the girls and drove them out of town. You said that Thomas took the first train north to look for her."

"It's not the whole story. I changed the truth as time passed. And now I'm changing it back again. No, not the truth, I guess that can never change. It's the facts then—I can change them back again."

"Well, you said that Thomas came back after three weeks looking for her and that he looked terrible—like Death himself. That only time cured him, and, of course, Ruth."

"Bob, do you think Tom Fine had a happy life?"

"Yes, I would say so. As happy as anyone who saw these parts tamed. It must have been lonely at times, but he had Ruth until five years ago, and they always seemed content out there on the farm. Yes, I'd say he had a long and contented life."

"Yes. Contented and long." Franz Kohler takes a deep breath and looks at the young reporter from the *Forest Leaves,* as if noticing him for the first time. "What you said happened is true. Thomas did return after three weeks. Of course, the respectable people would not answer his questions even if they knew, and the others just thought he was some crazy lumberjack. Which maybe he was. And, yes, time did cure him eventually. And Ruth."

"Then what is changed?"

"The one truth that has made my heart heavy with responsibility—a burden that made me forget and now makes me remember again. The one fact I never told Tom Fine. That his red-haired dream—Audrey, I believe her name was—is buried in an unmarked grave not fifty yards from his beloved Ruth."

"But you said that she went away—back East—after finding Thomas had left town."

"That's the story I told young Thomas Fine when he returned with nothing but an ounce of hope, because someone had told him that she had returned to Sherman looking for some lumberjack. She did return, two days after he had left town. The true events, lost to memory after so many years, come back to me now. How she returned badly beat up and sat in the station with no place to go.

"Her face was in a bad way, and even if it wasn't, no one in that town would have even acknowledged her presence, much less helped her. I told her that Thomas had headed north toward Seney in a crazy state looking for her. I told her that I didn't think he'd be back and that she should take the first train back north. She just sat on the wood bench and stared, not saying a word. She had this bag, and I assumed, after those several nights, she had enough money in it to take care of herself. I was young and thought that money itself could take care of someone, and that she'd even have her rewards after leaving that obese madam. These things came to me with experience, as did the ability to forget. So, at twenty, I left her alone to sit in the station and wait for the next train to take her back to Thomas. I was even young enough to picture them meeting and joining—two lonely people in this lonely country—in love's wild embrace.

"I was standing outside the hotel an hour later when we heard the scream. A woman who was passing through on the 8:12 found her lying dead, her wrists cut, beside a broken window in the ladies room. Those floorboards were fresh off the sawmill then so her blood left a dark stain that I'm sure is there to this day."

The two men—the young reporter and the aged lumberjack—sit quiet a moment, in reverence of time and story.

"Franz, why don't you let me tell it, for the paper? The true story of

Thomas Fine? They have a right to it, to the history."

"They have a right, as you put it, to the facts of what they pretty much already know, and if any wish to imagine anything more, that's their right too. Just the birth day, the death day, and ten lines of what they expect for everything in between. Print those things, Bob. What was, the past, exists regardless, and always will."

Celebration

The animal had come too far out of the woods. In a frozen instant the earth shook. The unknown mass flashed by in a direction opposite its beginning. It left at that spot, in that moment, an unknown noxious odor and the trailing off of thunder in a way that thunder does not trail off. The animal knew it as a warning because it did not make sense. Its mass and speed did not frighten as a gun cocked to explode frightens the human victim because of the face and twitching fingers belonging to the gun. It was not a springing wildcat. This thing was dangerous because it was outside the patterned principles of knowledge contained in the small, furry body. The Change of Things, through ions of time existent but never fully lived, was somehow recorded in its tiny being. Maybe just the beast's great-great-grandfather had seen it, come to know it—too short a time to be understood by the primordial record. The animal recorded the smell and sound in the unconscious hope that its descendants would know and understand. Then it turned and, in the same swift movement, bounded back into the pathless and ageless forest.

TRACY CULPEPPER FELT that she deserved this vacation. It had been four years to the day since her husband had taken her beyond the confines of their comfortable Chicago neighborhood. That had been their honeymoon, and they had driven a brand new Cadillac all the way to Niagara Falls and back. They had spent six nights at the Wedding Bells Motor Court on an interstate near the Falls and six carefree days enjoying the sights.

Drake had treated her to the best, and they had a marvelous time doing all the things one did and described on a three-by-five picture postcard signed "Wish you were here." One night they had dined late in a newly constructed tower that overlooked the Falls under colored floodlights. Drake put dimes in the Tourist Observation Telescopes, which made everything on the pavement seem like you were right down there. There were no Observation Telescopes on one side, but you could see many factories under orange smoke clouds. One day Drake heard someone say that a young boy in a boat had been helplessly swept over the precipice. It was a world very different from their Chicago, yet built of the same form and material. The eternal roar of water crashing on rocks had become a symbol of power, and the electricity it generated lit the floodlights which made the Falls pretty for the tourists.

Tracy had had a wonderful time that week. She was now again enjoying herself as the scenery of the northern Wisconsin forest flew by. She had never seen so many trees; the odor of balsam, Norway, cedar, and other varieties of pine mixed in pure air and entered the open window of the car.

"Drake, my hair is mussing. Close your window?"

"I'm sorry, honey, the air conditioning is broke."

"I thought you got it fixed."

"There wasn't time. Your hair is fine. I don't care if it's a little mussed and neither will Mr. Dawson."

She smiled. "You mean real estate men are all alike?"

"We see past certain things to be practical," Drake replied. "Enjoy the scenery. Have you ever seen such a beautiful forest?"

At that moment, Tracy jumped forward. A bee, caught in the air stream of the car, was sucked through the open window.

"There's a *bee* in here, Drake!"

"It's okay, Trace. Open your window and it will get out. It won't hurt you."

"Have you ever been stung by one?" she asked, frantically trying to hit the right button to open the window.

"No."

"Never?!"

"Nope. Never."

Tracy stared at her husband. She wondered how many people had never been stung by a bee. Maybe most people never had. Maybe she believed most people had because she had. She remembered the park when she was twelve and her poor father and the lonely picnic with egg salad sandwiches. Her father yelled, "Tracy, don't bite!" but too late. She had bitten the egg salad sandwich to which a bee had been attracted. She was stung on the inner lip. It had been one of the most horrible experiences of her life.

She looked around. The bee was trying to escape through the solid clarity of a backseat window.

"Well, I hope it stings you!"

However, the bee soon found the front escape portal, and left the car five minutes after its mistaken entry. It circled in confusion twice, then flew straight for the trees where it began going about its business as if nothing had happened. Actually, nothing had. It had gone five miles from Point A to Point B. To the bee, it didn't matter.

ON THE CANADIAN PRAIRIES towns grew at fairly regular intervals along the railroad at grain stations that were, at first, identified alphabetically. Man, however, cannot love a letter, and we have a need to love our creations. A, B, C became Aberdeen, Bruno, and Clair. Some did not survive and holes appeared in the pattern. Zelda eventually lost out to Yellow Creek.

Similarly, towns in the Wisconsin wilderness grew according to the patterns of water power, timber harvests, good glacial loess soil for potato farming, train stops, and ultimately the township-range system.

A network of highways connected the towns as a kind of vector force.

From an airplane it is easier to see that we are creatures of patterns. But ask a townsman, especially an elder citizen, and he will tell you that God chose the place for his community, and, as for the town fifteen miles up the road, we're gonna walk right over them Saturday night 'cause my boy Johnny's on the varsity this year. Which is probably good, for we are in need of smaller patterns.

THE CULPEPPER AUTOMOBILE entered Sherman and, after Drake stopped to ask directions from an indifferent gas-station attendant, found the South Lake Chain Road that would take them to the Twin Pines Inn, where they were to meet Mr. Sam Dawson. The road wove between numerous shimmering blue lakes, surrounded by white birch and majestic pine. Occasionally, a stretch of residences, each with its own driveway and dock, occurred. However, much of the way was still thick forest, which pleased the soul, no matter what the thoughts or schemes of the beholder.

The truth was, Drake Culpepper loved his wife. No matter what he did in his everyday life, it was that love that was the sum of his being. The rest of the world existed in a strange reality that was dealt with in whatever way he was supposed to deal with it. If he signed a paper that would cause acres of trees to be torn out with the roots by powerful machines, it was something he simply did so he could be with Tracy. In a world he found devoid of reason for action, she was his only justification for being.

And Tracy loved her husband, though it was a different kind of love, as every love no doubt is. Her love was that of a well-fed cat for the kind, old lady who has taken it in. She had once been very poor; now, she was well off and she loved Drake for what he was. Of course, that was only part of it. But in the complexity of their relationship it was a very important part; in the absence of a strong whole, a portion may dominate. She had asked him to take her along on this business trip so that she could see all those wonderful things that he found to be the nonessential debris of life. He readily agreed for her simple talk was his safety; her laugh a reassurance that the world only existed in what he felt for her.

The car pulled off the road onto the dusty gravel driveway of the Twin Pines Inn, a trail of dust lingering behind as they came to a halt in the parking area.

The Inn was an old log structure, well built and dark stained. Two huge white pines stood monumentally on the parking lot side. A cool, intoxicating breeze came off the lake, which was a million glittering jewels in the afternoon sun.

"It's beautiful," Tracy said.

Drake suddenly took her hand and pulled her along. They went down to the shore and walked out on the wooden dock, stopping at the end, although it seemed they were still moving as the waves below sought the shore. A powerboat with two young water skiers began to make a sweep of the lake.

"Look," Drake said, still holding her hand. She saw the skiers and he saw her eyes smile.

They turned and walked back to shore, their shadows before them in the water, becoming liquid. Slate steps led up the hill to the screen door of the Inn. Drake opened it and followed Tracy inside.

The inside was warm and friendly. The walls were varnished popple log. The bartender nodded at them and continued talking to his two plaid-shirted customers. They walked on the hardwood floor of the dining room, choosing a table by a dormant fireplace. It could have been a nineteenth-century inn where the stagecoach stopped.

A family with two young boys comprised the only other guests.

"I guess Mr. Dawson isn't here yet," Drake said, thinking, *I wish he would never arrive but then it would have to be something else.* "I'm sorry this has to be business, Trace."

"Honey, I'm having a wonderful time. I don't know what you *do* every day. This is exciting! I'm looking forward to meeting your Mr. Dawson."

"So am I," Drake replied automatically. "If this deal goes down, Mr. Sommer will be very pleased, which for us could mean that place on Oliver Street."

"I'm so happy," Tracy said, and she was.

The waitress came to their table, wearing a green calico dress with puffy short sleeves and a white apron. She was a high-school student from Sherman who worked at the Inn summers, trying to save enough money to leave Sherman in order to study to be a nurse down at Madison.

"Can I help you?"

They were looking at the menu. "Yes, umm—" Drake began. To Tracy, "Mr. Dawson said he comes here for the duck." He looked at the waitress. "We'll have the Northwoods Duck. Oh and bring a bottle of your best champagne. With three glasses."

"Thank you," said the girl, taking the menus away.

"Mr. Dawson says he comes here often," Drake offered, "For the duck."

"It's different," Tracy answered. "Nice."

The champagne arrived and Drake filled two glasses. They held the wine and Drake looked into his wife's eyes, which reflected the light from a window.

The toast: "To the best wife a man could hope to find. Happy Anniversary."

"Thank you, dear. You've made me happy." The champagne tingled in her nose.

"Mr. Culpepper?"

A man stood beside their table. He was of average height and wore a blue suit that fit precisely, as if the body were also tailored. The medium length, light-brown hair was trimmed neatly above the ears. The face smiled within an angular frame.

"Mr. Dawson! Pleased to meet you," Drake stood to shake his hand. "I'd like you to meet my wife, Tracy."

"Mrs. Culpepper, Tracy, I'm pleased to meet you." He bent to take her hand and their eyes met, examining. There was something felt by each when he momentarily held her delicate hand, but it was quickly ignored. Her eyes fell to his blue suit.

"Well, Mr. Dawson—" Drake began.

"Sam. Call me Sam."

"Sam, then, please join us." He poured another glass of champagne, as Sam Dawson sat down. "We're celebrating tonight."

Taking the champagne and smiling, "Oh, what's the celebration?"

"Today, Tracy and I have been married four years."

"Well, congratulations and best wishes for many more," turning to Tracy, still smiling.

"Thank you," Tracy said. She watched him closely and noticed a shiny gold ring with a black stone.

"In that case we won't discuss business tonight." Sam Dawson said, pausing, thinking. "I was just reminded that it would have been our anniversary soon."

"Oh, I'm sorry."

"Don't be. We were divorced. I wanted to work up here and she wouldn't leave Chicago."

"Then you're from the city?" Tracy asked.

"Oh, yes, originally."

"Do you like it up here?"

"Well, you know, I'm the outdoors type. Hunting, fishing, snowmobiling. I still get to the city occasionally, you know, mostly business. Take in a good show. But living here in the wilds just kind of keeps you on course. I couldn't go back."

The words said little, but the voice carried a nuance, an implication, meant to build a certain potential validity to complement the blue suit, and she was the only woman at the table.

"Speaking of nature, this is very pretty country and my firm would be interested in helping to develop its recreational potential," Drake began as he thought he should, his life secure beside him.

Sam Dawson turned from Tracy. "Well that's great, Drake. Our firm has been looking for some new blood in this area—you know, it has a lot to offer. Did you know that on some of these lakes frontage rates have been increasing about 30 percent each year? That's right. And, Lord knows, things are only looking up."

"Sounds promising. In our correspondence you indicated you were willing to have us—"

"We need fresh Chicago ideas, and, frankly, capital investment. And since we have acquired or are in the process of acquiring much of the land around Sherman, I believe we have the grounds for a viable agreement," Sam Dawson smiled. He glanced toward Tracy. "But enough business for now."

The waitress appeared and carefully placed the plates before the customers, Northwoods Duck all around.

"Susan, tell your father I said hello."

"I will, Mr. Dawson." A quick smile and she left.

"Susan's father is a friend of mine. Owns a boat rental place over on Long Lake. He's appreciative of our work up here. Helps business, of course. Makes you feel good to know you're helping a community." He noticed Tracy's eyes were still on the girl. "Ed worries about Susan. She seems determined to move away. He thinks she's watching too much TV," dismissing the thought with a wave of the hand. "I don't know, some of these kids."

They all ate, attempting to avoid talking about business and trying to find topics for conversation. They agreed that the food was very good. Drake and Sam Dawson discussed restaurants in Chicago and Milwaukee.

Tracy had been quietly eating, watching and listening intently.

"Mr. Dawson," she began.

"Sam."

"Sam, I've lived my whole life in the city, and this is very nice, but there aren't many people and ... things, you know, up here. I can understand how that girl might be bored, growing up here and all."

He looked at Drake's pretty, blonde wife. "Well Tracy, you get to know people—there are more than it seems—and there are nice places to go. Resorts and clubs that are really as good as anything in the city."

Drake interrupted, "We're staying at the Northern Star in Eagle Creek."

"That's a good example," Sam Dawson continued. "Go to the lounge there on any night while you're here and meet the people. I think you'll like it. It's like the city except there aren't, well, so many people you don't know... or need to know." He watched as she drank her champagne and lifted his own glass, not knowingly planning what he would do, other than that everything he did was in accordance with a few simplistic motives. When the check came, he insisted on paying it.

"Well, fine," Drake said. "But we owe you one."

"I hope to see a lot of you and Tracy."

"Likewise. We will," Drake answered in confusion, for his business life and his real life had been strangely entwined during the evening in a distasteful distortion of champagne and something else he would never understand.

"Well, Drake, this was a start, but you probably want to talk with the main office anyway. Tell you what. I've got a great idea. Tomorrow, come to the office—it's on Timberline Lake—and while you talk with my higher-ups, I'll take Tracy fishing, just off the dock, and when you're ready just come down and wave and we'll pick you up and we'll all try to catch some of the big fish we've got in these lakes."

"That sounds wonderful. I was afraid Tracy might be bored."

"I'm afraid of worms," Tracy blurted.

"Oh, we won't use worms. A spinning reel and a silver spoon should be right for you." She like the sound of the words.

"I'd best leave you two on your special day." He rose to say goodbye, taking Tracy's hand. Something was again felt, now with more knowledge, less quickly ignored. "It was a great pleasure meeting you, Tracy."

"Likewise. I'm looking forward to tomorrow."

"Drake," shaking his hand firmly, "Pleased to do business with you."

"It's been a pleasure. I look forward to discussing our interests in more detail. Thank you for dinner."

"Not at all. 'Til tomorrow then."

Sam Dawson turned and walked to the door, casually waving to the bartender. Tracy watched the blue suit disappear through the screen door.

"He seems a genial fellow," Drake said.

"Yes, he does." Tracy looked at her husband. She felt a sudden surge of love for him, touched with melancholy and vague images of the past. It was like a gasp for air. She smiled. "I'm sure he'll make a good business connection."

They sat and finished the bottle of champagne, occasionally making jokes about a mounted buck's head a taxidermist had skillfully prepared for the Inn. Tracy laughed heartily at the jokes, for the hidden thought of fishing tomorrow with Sam Dawson mixed excitement with the humor. Drake listened to her laugh and was happy for the moment and forever because he knew that was all there was.

"Let's catch the show at the Northern Star," he said.

AS THEY STEPPED OUTSIDE, it was still warm and the breeze rustled the birch leaves, revealing their silvery bottoms. The lake burned brightly in the late afternoon sun. Some children played on an offshore diving raft and their shouts came clearly over the water. An old man fished from the dock, slowly reeling in.

Drake and Tracy hurried to their Cadillac and sped away in the dust that lingered, suspended in the still between afternoon and evening. The bartender saw them leave and shook his head. The tires squealed on the Lake Chain Road as they raced toward Highway X, the vector which would take them back to Eagle Creek.

"Only You Can Prevent Forest Fires," Drake read a sign post off the road by a stand of Norway pine. Tracy laughed. Now, many tall, straight Norway flew by the low, orange sun, which did not move, keeping pace with the speeding auto. Then, cool shadow totally engulfed the road as it headed away from the lake. Moments later another lake appeared and was left behind. Then another appeared. The road turned into the sun and lakes were now on both sides.

The car raced on, through woods calm and peaceful with age, past an old man walking on the shoulder, thinking, *They'll go faster and faster. Better slow down, the curve—*

"Do you think we'll see a deer?" Tracy yelled.

"Of course, *dear.*"

She laughed at the simple pun. Drake listened, staring at the highway. Her laugh filled the car. It filled everything. He thought he noticed something different about it. He listened to the memory of the laugh. No, it was the same. He listened to the memory again. It was beautiful. The wine seemed to have enabled him to listen to the memory indefinitely.

The sun shone through a clearing in the trees straight ahead, although the road turned away in darkness. Drake, listening, remembering, saw just the clearing, that part of his mind accepting an illusion of dusk. The wheel in his hand did not turn. The tires threw pebbles, the road banked away, the tires not turning. The shiny, metallic bumper clipped off a guard post. Shaking and scratching as bushes and branches scraped the sides. The laugh quickly stopped. Remembering, thinking, *what's happening?* Quick, dull scraping of surprise turning to terror. Then nothing. Then thump and splash of absurd water. She screamed because he heard it but not understanding *What is happening? and her screaming I heard her laugh that's not right Water?* And she screaming at him for help and he not understanding but frantically trying to unbuckle the seat belt. *That isn't right* the scream and her clawing *No!* He pushed her away and the screaming stopped her head becoming limp in the rising water *I'm sorry* and the seat belt *Why doesn't she move* and the seat belt now under water rising *Just not right not what was happening Tracy!* The seat belt undone *C'mon Trace!* and the water too high and he didn't understand that other thing *Why is it doing this?* and holding Tracy tight trying to yell *I'm sorry* and "I'm sorry" in a gasp a bubble as the lake water filled his lungs.

On the surface, oil and gasoline, refined remnants of green, living plants millions of years dead, rose and fell, covering the small swells in various colors of the rainbow.

LINCOLN DERBY WAS TOO old to run. He walked along the shoulder of the Lake Chain Road and Highway X from early morning until past sundown, holding his one bad hand in the good one. Townsfolk were always glad to see him and waved as they passed. No one really knew why he walked the roads, but it made them feel comfortable and good. People from out of town would think him strange, or more likely not see him at all. But the townspeople loved him for his presence. Some older folks remembered a tragedy and that he had lived in seclusion for years, but that was a long time ago—long enough to be forgotten by the collective memory of the town.

Lincoln walked faster, thinking, *I'm getting too old to run and what would I do? Take off my clothes and try to rescue them? I'm an old man, too old to be a hero.* He reached the spot where the car had flown off the road. Nothing. *Only a trace of oil to mark the obscurity of a grave.* He turned with his head downcast, walking slowly across the road to a small, white frame cottage and knocked lightly on the door. *Faster and faster,* his mind repeating.

The door opened. A middle-aged man in a sport shirt said, "Yes?"

"I'd like to use your telephone. There's been an accident down the road."

The man looked annoyed. "Alright, follow me." He led the old man through a shiny plastic kitchen. "There," he said pointing at the wall.

A dial was in the handle part and Lincoln spun it carefully seven times.

"Hello, Sheriff? Lincoln Derby."

"Well, hey Linc! How's things? Beautiful day, hey?"

"One of the best. Jim, I just saw a bad one. Couple Chicago folk flew right off the road. I didn't see anyone come out."

"Christ! Where?"

"Timberline. The deep channel by the road, on the south end. You know, right where old Tom Fine caught that prize walleye last year."

"Damn! When will those people get some sense? Did you see the plates?"

"Just a glimpse.. but they was Chicago folk."

"Well, okay, thanks Lincoln. We'll check it out. Have to get the big winch up from Elksburgh in the morning." He paused. "Say, you comin' to the Fireman's Picnic Sunday?"

"Have I missed one in twenty years?"

"Good. Good. My boy Johnny's gonna win that greased-pole event. Came close last year."

"Tell Grace I'm looking forward to her blueberry pie."

"I will. She'll be glad you said so." After another short pause, "By the way, Linc, do you know what Tom's walleye hit? Need some new luck."

"Meppes four, I believe."

"Hmm. Well, thanks again, Lincoln. We'll get right on that. And see you Sunday."

"Goodbye."

Lincoln hung up, thanked the man in the sport shirt, and walked back outside. The sun would soon set, and the entire sky over the far shore was a brilliant, burning orange that faded into a cool, transparent blue. Things became well-defined and sharply intense in the orange light: a burning up of moments in the grandest of endings. Then, coolness, the North Star and Venus, mosquitoes and bats in silhouette, and warm lights from the cottage windows. People inside, safe from the night, with memories of today and hopefully a thought for tomorrow—unconsciously aware that their sleep must end in the bright, brisk beginning called morning.

Lincoln Derby buttoned the old wool Pendleton jacket and walked down the road, thinking, *There's enough day left to get to the new bridge going up at the Thoroughfare.* He walked, holding the bad hand in the good one. A picture of the new bridge came to mind. He wanted to see how much work had been done in a day's time.

The Inner Tube Race

"All contestants down to the dock!"

Eve Scalworthy called as she looked at her watch. Scattered groups of tourists and townspeople assembled quite solemnly, as if for the beginning of Sunday's service. Eve turned to Jean Oberling, whose son had won the race last summer, and remarked, "Tommy should win easily, Jean. There's no competition this year."

"What about Jill Latimore?"

Both women chuckled. Jill was the first girl to compete in Sherman's inner tube race.

"Now, Jean, don't you think it's about time we women were represented? I think it's wonderful. I even gave the young lady the responsibility of passing out the equipment." She turned to the contestants, who were preparing for the mile-and-a-half trek to the east end of Jewel Lake at the highway bridge.

"Hurry! I won't have this be our first rained-out event."

The morning had been sunny and warm, although a strong wind etched whitecaps on the sky-blue lake. A cloud passed turning the lake steel gray, only to again become the deceptive blue with the sun's return. Dark thunderheads waited ominously on the western horizon.

Mr. Scalworthy, owner of the Lost Bungalow Resort which sponsored the race, was about to fire the starting gun when Jill, who was distributing the paddles, vocalized what some others had noticed.

"Scott's not here yet."

They all agreed to wait for the fourteen-year-old Scott, who lived farther from town than most of the boys. Sally Whitestone, Scott's mother, remained unmentioned. Sally was a widow who had been married to a Chippewa Indian who had died in an accident at the mill. Sally was attractive and pleasant, and men, for the most part, addressed her politely and with respect. Lately there had been whispering that Sally was keeping private company with George Latimore, the town's postmaster. As George and his wife, Emma, and daughter, Jill, stood waiting in the midst of the crowd, people became uncomfortable. Eve suggested they begin anyway because of the threatening rain.

"I think we should wait for Scott," Jill insisted.

Emma Latimore had had a few drinks up at the lodge and George was anxious to get on with the event.

"We can't hold up the race, Jill," he said.

But as he spoke they heard the old pick-up truck and knew it was Sally Whitestone's. Scott came running down the hill to the shore and Sally, in jeans and a blue wind-breaker, followed. She looked for Eve.

"I'm sorry we're late. Some trouble with the truck."

"No problem, Sally," Eve assured her. "Let's go Scotty. You've got some tough competition here!"

Scott looked at Jill and smiled. All the racers lined up with their feet in the water.

Mr. Scalworthy lifted the pistol, which he had spent two hours at Lyle's Sporting Goods picking out but which he used just once each year at this event, and fired a shot that the wind blew immediately still. The youths ran splashing into the lake until they were deep enough to jump awkwardly onto the inner tubes and start paddling. It was a good, clean start with all contestants digging furiously into the waves.

"Go Tommy!" Eve yelled.

Someone else yelled, "C'mon Jill! Show 'em what us girls can do!"

Sally watched Scott until he merged with the others and then glanced at George, who stood beside his wife. He smiled as their eyes met briefly.

"So anyone for a cocktail?" Emma suggested loud enough to be heard by all.

"Wait 'til they round the point. Then we'll drive over to the finish line," George countered.

Sally stood alone, not knowing what to do with herself. No one offered to relieve the burden of her isolation. Eve and Jean Oberling were discussing a matter concerning the Legion dance to be held Saturday night. Sally studied Emma for a moment. George's wife was about five years her senior: a slim brunette with sharp features, wearing a stylish pant suit. She was from the East, as was George, and everyone knew she disliked Sherman, Wisconsin. Sally pictured the handwritten note she had received that morning:

Dear Sally,

Try to avoid the inner tube race. See if Scott can catch a ride. Emma will be there— she'll no doubt have started early.

I will talk with her today. I love you. George

Sally was about to turn when Emma caught her eye and began to walk toward her. George followed quickly behind.

"Hello, Sally. How are you? We don't get to see you often."

"I'm fine, thank you, Emma."

"What have you been doing with yourself since, well—"

"Since Billy died? Oh, I've just been trying to manage. Surely Jill keeps you informed."

"Yes, it's so nice that our children are friends."

Sally looked at George who was suffering silently.

"Hello, Sally," he said.

"Hello, George."

"Well, isn't this nice—to get together on such an occasion as this."

With this sardonic note from Emma, Sally turned to look for the racers. They were all bunched together about a quarter mile across the bay, nearing the point.

"Your Scott is a strong boy," Emma said. "He should finish well."

"Yes. He sure gets a lot of exercise," Sally responded.

George looked perplexed from woman to woman to the lake.

"He is a fine young man," he mumbled.

Eve Scalworthy interrupted. "It looks like rain. Quick! Let's everybody get over to the bridge and meet the winners."

And so the gathering dispersed, to reassemble at the east end of Jewel Lake. The Latimores did not leave immediately, however. The rain had begun, lightly at first, before George persuaded Emma to leave the bar.

"ARE YOU SURE HE GOT the cracked paddle?" Scott yelled as they neared the point.

Jill paddled close.

"He got it. I made sure there was some tape over the crack."

Tommy Oberling was paddling like a steam locomotive and was sufficiently in the lead, already rounding the bend. Scott and Jill were with the pack, well behind.

"It should go in these waves. The tape totally covered it but I cracked it good."

Moments later they noticed Tommy's arms stop pumping. Then he raised the broken paddle into the air in helpless defiance, bobbing steadily like a marker buoy.

"What rotten luck," Jill said, laughing.

THE CROWDED FIELD BEGAN to pass Tommy now. Having jettisoned the useless paddle, he had jumped into the water and was trying to swim with one arm around the buoyant float.

"We'll send the boat to pick you up," Scott yelled.

"It's not fair!" Tommy spit out a mouthful of lakewater. "Jill. Lend me your paddle! C'mon! You won't finish anyway."

"Sorry Tommy," Scott answered as he passed.

"Shut your mouth you half-breed!"

Both Jill and Scott laughed as they passed the helpless object of their fun and rounded the point into the channel between the two lakes. Almost a mile remained now across a choppy Jewel Lake. It was starting to rain, but not very hard at first.

"Scott, do you really want to win this?" Jill asked, trying to catch her breath.

"No. Do you?"

"No, of course not. I just entered to represent my sex. Slow down. At least we won't be last."

They stopped the hard, steady stroking of the water and allowed their peers to gain distance.

"Look what I've got."

Jill was wearing a T-shirt, now soaked through. From its pocket she removed a waterproof wrapping. Inside she found two dry cigarettes and matches. She gave one to Scott.

"Here."

"We are bad today, hey?"

Jill lit the cigarettes carefully, and they puffed as if discovering some dark secret of growing up. Scott inhaled the smoke.

Jill tried a deeper drag.

"Scott?" She exhaled.

"Yeah?"

"I think my parents are breaking up."

"Yeah."

"I think, I mean, I have a feeling that they are going to get divorced."

"Soon?"

"I think so."

They were drifting now, toward the bridge and the people, the wind blowing the rain against their backs. The rain brought with it a steady drop in temperature. They paddled, slowly.

Scott looked at her. He shivered as his body cooled.

"You know what will happen then."

"Yes."

"Your mother will go away."

She nodded.

"And you will stay. With your father." He said this, not asked. "He will marry my mother. Probably soon afterward. I know she would agree."

"Yes." Jill watched him. She held the cigarette between her lips, the wind blowing the smoke from her eyes.

"And me and you—" He halted.

"Will be brother and sister."

He looked at her. They bobbed together, in unison, as they rode the same waves. Her short, brown hair was wet and matted. Water dropped from the fresh, tanned cheeks. The sky was dark gray. The wind bent the tree-tops along the shore.

"Yes," Scott said. "You will be my sister." He looked into her eyes, thinking. He laughed shortly, not laughing.

She removed the cigarette from her lips.

"What's so funny?"

"You know. I'll be your brother."

"Oh. Well."

What happened next was only inexplicable to him later when he recalled it. He would grin then, remembering, no longer fourteen. Now it came pure and inevitable as the cold, summer rain that pushed them toward the finish.

He leaned over his inner tube and held hers close. She did not move, waiting. Their lips came together softly but fully, awkwardly, and wet in the rain. Both closed their eyes without knowing that they had done so. It was a test, simple and eloquent in its innocence. He sat back, still holding her inner tube.

"Well?" he asked finally.

She giggled. "I think you could take some lessons from Ilene Schneider."

"What do you think?" she asked, now serious.

"I think I can beat you to the bridge."

WHEN THEY FINISHED, he a few yards ahead of her, and were again on firm ground, pictures were already being taken. Ken Braun had won in their division and Joe Meinzer in the senior division. A boat that was about to pass beneath the bridge was sent back to pick up an outraged Tommy Oberling. Scott and Jill smiled at this news.

Parents applauded the winners as Eve Scalworthy watched with binoculars the rescue of young Tommy with the nervous and embarrassed Oberlings.

George Latimore hurried Jill off to their car, where Emma waited.

"See you tomorrow, Scott," Jill yelled.

Scott walked through the mud, which felt good in its firm support, to the truck where his mother waited.

"Well, how'd it go, Scotty?" Sally asked. "Did you win?"

"No. But neither did Tommy. Matterafact, he came in last. His paddle broke."

"Oh?" Sally started the truck. "How did Jill do?"

"Real good. I only beat her by inches."

"Yes, she is a strong girl."

The thunderstorm hit hard as people were arriving home from the race. It snapped and crashed with a terrible cacophony, and lightning shattered the dark sky in tangled webs of piercing light.

Jill spent the evening in her room listening to the storm and reading a book she had bought at Medford's. Occasionally her mind drifted to thoughts about the summer. Yes, it had been fine so far. Scott was a good friend. She liked him better than her girlfriends. He seemed more real, and honest. She liked to go fishing with him, and on Saturday nights they went to the picture show.

The thunder gradually became muted and distant. Soon Jill heard the voices of her parents. They were once again arguing over something. The voices became louder, replacing the sounds of the departing storm.

After a few minutes, Jill jumped to her feet and walked toward the stairs. They were downstairs, beyond the hall and pocket doors of the living room. She slowly descended until she stood outside the doors. She was in her pajamas. The voices were loud now.

"So you think I drink too much, do you, George?"

"Everyone knows you drink too much."

"Oh, everyone knows. You mean, of course, everyone in this little town knows. Well let me tell you something, George. This isn't exactly the world, is it? *Is it?* Some folks know enough to leave a person's private life be. Of course, they are a bit more sophisticated."

"I think folks here have been very kind to you."

"Kind?!" Jill heard her mother's mocking laugh. "Kind? Sure, on Main Street. In daylight. Kind? Bullshit, George. Do you know what they're saying right now, in their homes or down at Jerry's? And not just about me, dear. I'm sure they've caught wind —'caught wind?' My God! I'm beginning to talk like them!—I'm sure their postmaster's little fling with our poor, helpless widow Sally Whitestone is being mentioned in hushed tones."

"That's a different subject, Emma."

"Oh, no. Sally has been what we've been talking about all along, she's been the subject of these discussions long before we moved here. Sally, or the possibility or threat—call it what you want, you're the talker—the threat of her then, has been it since—. Don't look at me that way, George. I'm not the only one in this room whose hands are shaking."

There was a pause as Jill stood by the door. Then her father replied, slowly and quietly so Jill had to take a step closer:

"If I tremble it is because I've been trying to make a decision, trying to choose, carefully—no, not carefully. There has been too little use of the brain at all for that. But choosing nevertheless. And not just these past few months, but since I came into this world, unprepared as we all are, and nothing to help guide me. If I tremble, maybe it's because I need help, something to show me the way, something that doesn't exist in God or in alcohol or even perhaps in love."

"Well, well. How perfect. You know, George, you fit in just right here. You're as quaint as their Legion dances and firemen's picnics. Wait until they find you out." Her voice became more excited. "What choice do I have? They've seen to that, haven't they? They've accomplished what you might have found you didn't even want, what you might have discovered was a mistake, the wrong choice. Because of them, it's too late. Maybe I could have forgiven on my own, but—" She stopped. "I've lost Jill, too, haven't I?" Then this, like a hushed explosion: "Well, you can have your divorce... and take your squaw! I'm going back to New York where the hottest event in August isn't some juvenile inner tube race."

Jill turned from the door. Her head became light and her body still felt as if she rode up and down the unceasing waves of the afternoon. She returned to her room, the voices fading in the dark below. She was thinking of the County Fair to be set up next week just outside town. A smile came to her lips as she slipped into bed, beneath the thick quilt that was needed even now in mid-August. It became very quiet in the house. She saw in her mind one fall day before Thanksgiving as she walked home beside Scott down the middle of School Street, joking with him about a new teacher who didn't even know that Eagle Creek was their arch-rival in football.

Then, her lips moved, faintly, as if the momentary continuum of consciousness and sleep induced a catharsis; the thought, perhaps the hope, already silent with the speaking, addressed to the subconscious of the night:

"I will fall in love someday. And he will love me. We will be very, very happy."

An Intermission

I got scared of the smell and the closeness. It's like the bright picture in the sky except it's all around and small. Bright and small so I can't breathe and the smell of can't breathing. The white people talk at me like the moving picture when I'm near a noise box but like I can answer. The picture in the stars doesn't do that and the others just scream and I go away. But they took away the place that's all warm inside. I start to cry. Bright and all around and too close to breathe. Stop crying, now, they say, Stop crying, Jason. Like I'm all inside the bright picture and the stars are all gone...

THERE ARE FOLKS IN town who think I'm stupid, which I'm not. They are so smug it kills me. I didn't even marry a city boy and move away like all the other girls are doing. No, I'm still here in Sherman where I was born, but do you think that makes any difference to them? 'Course not, and I know why. It's because I married Lenny, and they don't like him or what we do either. I mean, our business. And then they blame me for Jason, too. Well, that's O.K. with me. I'd just as soon move to the Rez and live with Lenny's people.

But I don't think Lenny would like that. Anyway, I never talk about it. Lenny's got his own ways. We've been here in the lot almost eight years and so there ain't much chance of leaving. Anyway, we see the movies free.

Lenny loves the movies. He always has ever since he was ten and walked to town for the first time to see one. He told me it was a John Wayne movie where they shot all the crazy Indians. Lenny just loved that movie. Which is kinda strange when you think that Lenny's a Chippewa.

He said he wanted to go to Hollywood and be an Indian in the movies. I guess they never have enough of them. But he didn't have the money ever. So when he was eighteen he went into Rapids one Wednesday (that's when they get the new movies there—it's always Tuesday here) and waited to talk to the man who changes them. Mr. Gordon, our distributor now, said they needed someone capable to manage the Sherman Outdoor and that he would recommend him. Well, he did and Lenny got the job.

That's when I met him. I had come to the Outdoor with someone else, but I ended up with Lenny. Lenny kinda beat him up, too. I felt bad, but I'm like that. Lenny says it was during *The Good, the Bad, and the Ugly* with Clint Eastwood, but I don't remember myself.

So we got married. My parents wouldn't come or anyone for that matter. But I loved Lenny so I didn't care. I moved in with him in his trailer, which he's got set up at the back of the lot—near the refreshment stand and where they run the movie. Lenny runs the movies now since they showed him how. It's not hard, I guess. He says they just about go by themselves.

At first everything was real nice. We fixed up the trailer—got a color T.V., and Lenny put together a stereo system that's real loud. I tell him it's too loud for the size of the trailer. He plays it so loud in the morning when I take a walk that you can hear it out on the highway. Sometimes Mr. Derby asks what all the noise is when I meet him on the road. But he don't play it that loud when I'm at home. Then Lenny put in a special line from the booth and hooked it up so we can listen to the new movie on Tuesday night over the stereo speakers. We sit on the couch, which is set just right for watching the screen out the side window.

We watched all the big movies that year—sometimes more than a few times if they stayed on two weeks. That was real nice. But what I didn't realize was that all of a sudden the season ends. Just like that. They take away the movie and don't give you another. 'Course there's no people left after Labor Day. Just the town people, and they don't come much. Especially after of few tried to shut us down.

Lenny spent his time fixing the trailer for winter but he seemed to get a little down. I don't think he thought about the season ending either. I had to get a job at the grocery in town, which I didn't mind—I could get bored in that trailer all day long. Just before the first snowfall we drove down to Elksburg. Lenny bought about ten new record albums, and that seemed to cheer him up some.

We did all right that winter. It was kind of nice really. We even saved enough money to get a used snowmobile, which we still own. We drove it around the lot and all over. It got real cold, but we could keep it warm enough in the trailer that you could get by with a warm sweater. And at night we had each other, of course. That was really the best part of the winter.

Then before we thought much more about it the season began again. We got the first movies the Tuesday after Memorial Day. Had about thirty cars opening day too. But I could tell right away it was going to be different, when Lenny told me what to put on the marquee—there were no famous names, and I had to put up RATED X in the same size letters.

This part is kind of personal, but I figure I better include it because it's important. After Lenny set up the movie that night he came back with some popcorn like usual, and we got set to watch the show. Well, I never seen anything like that before on the screen. Lenny just sat there and stared. I tried to follow what was happening, but it didn't make any sense. Just all these naked people making love and doing some things I couldn't believe.

I tried to ask Lenny about it, but he told me to be quiet. After a while he got sort of wild and began taking my clothes off. I figured it would be better than watching the stupid movie, so I went along. But

Lenny was kinda crazy, and it was, well, different. I can honestly say that it had always been good with Lenny, but not that time. It was like I wasn't even there or something.

We didn't talk much the rest of the week. The girl who collects the money took off a couple days, so I took over in the booth. I was kind of mad at Lenny, anyway—the way he would stare at those naked girls. The movie was only scheduled for one week, so I thought things might get back to normal.

But when Lenny told me what to change the marquee to that next Tuesday, I almost cried. I can still remember putting up the letters, feeling about as low as a body could possibly feel. X-STACY & MILE HIGH SEX—RATED XXX. In front of our drive-in! I couldn't believe it.

That night the same thing happened. And then the next Tuesday, too, until I even began to get used to it. Like a schedule or something. But I was beginning to feel sad all the time. I wished they would give us the regular movies again.

Those movies took something from me somehow. Not that Lenny felt any less for me—I knew he loved me more than anything including movies—but some part of our marriage or maybe even a piece of me, myself, got lost each time he stared at those pictures. Because they all lied about it. That's what happened—they took what he truly felt for me and turned it into a lie. A lie that was maybe easier to believe in—easier to want—than the truth. But a stinking lie, anyway.

One day I went to the doctor at the hospital and found out I was pregnant. Actually, I sort of knew before that, but it's the kind of knowing that you don't really believe until someone else tells you, confirms it; then you sort of believe what you already knew. Lenny was happy, too, when I told him, which I was glad of because I thought he might get mad, although I really knew he wouldn't, but it was sort of like I just said about not believing what you already know.

Lenny began to treat me better then, although I don't want you to think he was treating me bad. We were both looking forward to the baby, so we had something to plan for. A couple movies stayed on a few weeks and Lenny gave his total attention to me for a while. We went shopping for things and drove to Wausau and back one day. It was real fine and I felt better about things.

We expected the baby in February. Lenny had trouble finding work for the winter and we ran kind of low on money. What do I mean kind of low? We did without food some days. Finally—and I don't know what we'd of done any later—he got work on the new school they were building in Eagle. Got paid pretty good, too, although I think it was "under the table" if you know what I mean. So for Christmas Lenny bought a beautiful crib for the baby and we were both so happy and proud, and I don't think we've ever loved each other more than that Christmas.

February came and I had the baby. It wasn't that simple, but the result is what counts and that appeared to be a healthy, seven pound twelve ounce boy. I thought he looked like Lenny but Lenny said he had my cute nose. I loved that baby as much as Lenny and I can truthfully say that I've never lost any of that love, although it's been hard. If anything I love that boy now more than ever.

The next season began and, except for the baby which took all my time, it turned out just like the year before. Lenny loved the baby, but he more and more began to treat me like a stranger or just an object. I hate to say these things about him because I know he loves me but it's what happened to him from watching those movies. I know a lot of wives live their whole lives like that and they don't even know that it's not right. But I remembered with all my soul how it used to be, so I knew there was a difference. By that time when we made love—no —when he decided to have me—I wasn't even there if you know what I mean. I might as well be any one of those women in the lot getting it from just any guy.

When Jason was over a year old, I began to worry about him but I wasn't sure why. He seemed to be not quite right somehow. I thought it was my imagination, which maybe it was—I've learned a lot of true things when I was just imagining. We took him to the hospital after a while and they did a bunch of tests and that was when they told us he was retarded. I got real scared because I didn't know exactly what that meant. There had been one girl in school who everyone picked on and they said she was retarded. I always felt sorry for her. I couldn't believe that my son could be like that. I thought about everybody making fun of that girl and didn't stop crying all the way home.

But we went back to talk with the doctor and I read some books about it and then I wasn't so scared. Lenny never said much but I knew that he was worried. But we loved Jason more than ever then. At first I was like I now know most people are and that's just ignorant. Jason is just like other kids—happy and healthy and full of love, but just not as smart as most. Well, I've found that "smart" people can really be ignorant about things they don't bother to understand.

Since then time has gone by almost before I knew it. Jason grew like a weed until he got almost as big as me and only seven years old. I spent most of my time caring for him, but I always took my morning walk while Lenny watched Jason. I'd go outside and smell the air and look out over the lot. All the cars from the night before would be gone and it was real dead but like it might come alive at any moment. All you could see where the cars had been were the poles that hold the speakers and it looked like the cars had simply gone underground and sent up periscopes to watch for it to start on the blank screen. As soon as they would see the first sign of it—all the tangled flesh and limbs—the cars would come back up and then all you'd see was the cars, all attentive and like they would jump at the screen any minute. But in the morning all you'd see was the watchful periscopes and the sun bleaching out the screen, like it was trying to burn out the sickness that lived on it each night.

Sometimes I'd try to pick up the garbage that would blow around in the morning. There'd be beer and soda cans, popcorn and candy boxes. Every now and then, when Jason was big enough, he'd go with me and pick up as much of the junk as he could. I didn't let him do that much though—it was bad enough I had to do it. Sometimes I'd find a used you-know-what along with the beer cans and stuff. But that was unusual. If people get that hot and heavy at a drive-in, well, they don't usually worry about using one of those.

So this is what happened. It was the first Saturday night after we opened this season. We had quite a few cars because the city people come up for a short vacation then and wanted their X-rated movies. Lenny had watched it when it came in and, like I said, things haven't changed much. So that Saturday night he was listening to the stereo with the headphones and I was watching TV. Jason was very active so I told him to go get popcorn. He liked to do that since we showed him how and it's real close by the trailer. Sometimes he came back without the popcorn and frightened, but I guess that's going to happen with ignorant people scaring him. He was always all right soon as he got back inside.

That night Jason must have decided to walk past the refreshment stand. He looked into the window of a car where this guy was getting it on with his girlfriend. Naturally, Jason was interested in what he was doing so he watched. Then the man saw him and started yelling. Jason was so confused and scared he couldn't move. He began to cry, louder and louder. People started honking their horns. I ran outside and Lenny followed.

My only interest was to reassure Jason, but while I was holding him this guy kept hollering. I didn't stay to listen, but he was repeating something about the owner and the police and getting us fired. We took Jason back to the trailer. We get threats all the time.

Well, it turned out this guy's real big in local real estate and has a lot of power around Sherman. The police came and some other town folk—those who had tried to shut us down—and Mr. Gordon. They told us either we "institutionalize" Jason or Lenny would lose his job. I cried all that week. If Lenny lost his job we'd be done for. And the doctor had been talking about putting Jason in an institution also. We didn't have any choice. They took Jason away from us that Sunday.

Something happened in the two weeks since I finished telling how they took Jason away. I still feel sort of bitter, but I have to change what I was going to say now because everything's changed.

It was last Tuesday. We had a new X-rated movie as usual. I felt real depressed, just looking at the stupid TV with the sound off. Lenny had the curtain open to watch the movie and the sound on but when I looked he was just sort of staring like in a daze. After a while he turned the sound off. I got up to look at the screen. There were the usual bunch of entwined, naked bodies. I noticed the picture was a little dark and I figured that was why I had heard some people honking their horns. I was about to tell Lenny about it when someone began pounding on the door.

I opened it and there was a fat, bald-headed man wearing a flashy sport shirt.

"You run this place?" he demanded.

I looked around at Lenny and the man saw him.

"What the hell's the matter with you? Can't you hear everyone? You blind or what? I didn't pay five bucks to look at a dark screen!"

Lenny just stared at him.

"Answer me! Are you deaf?"

Lenny didn't answer but something snapped in me.

"No, he ain't deaf," I said. "Or blind. He just don't see no reason to listen to a jerk like you. What gives you the right to bust in on us and demand anything? Just 'cause you probably got more money than we'll ever have? Is that it? You think you're so respectable and we're just scum, huh? Well, let me tell you something, mister. We don't think much of you or your money or your so-called respectability. We got something you'll never understand 'cause you're too... What's happened

to you, your senses that you gotta come here for... for that? You're the one that's sick, not my son or—"

I felt Lenny's hand on my shoulder. I was crying.

"Get out," Lenny said.

"I'm leaving," the man said. "But your wife just caused you a lot of trouble, boy!"

Lenny shut the door. My face was on his chest making it wet. He smiled at me and said, "Come here." I stopped crying. We were at the bed and he was taking off my clothes—gently. I took off his shirt and then we got under the covers. We hugged each other tight for a long time. Then, we made love and it was as nice as it always used to be.

After a while Lenny got up to take care of the movie. I just lay there thinking and feeling good but real tired. I was still shocked that I said those things to a customer.

Then Lenny returned and he was smiling. He came back to bed. That's when he said it:

"Start packing tomorrow."

"What?" I said, screamed.

"I'm quitting this job. We're leaving."

"But where can we go? What will you do?" I couldn't believe he was serious.

"My uncle can get me a job at the pulp mill. We'll live on the Rez. I know just the spot. It's on a cleared hill by the woods. My family owns the land. In the woods there's a pretty stream, closer than we are to the road here. I'll catch the trout in the stream. You'll take care of Jason—"

"Jason?" I screamed.

He looked at me and I remember thinking that he suddenly looked alive.

"We'll be on Indian land," he said. "Nobody can take the son of Ojibwe and put him in a white-man's institution."

So I'm leaving Sherman. Like I said, that's fine with me. Don't get me wrong—I've grown up here and I've had as many good times as anyone. And there are good people here. I'll miss Mr. Derby and Mr. Latimore at the post office. But Sherman isn't just those good things. Just like anywhere else, I guess, there's people here who don't understand that we just have to live, too. But I see now that we have something they don't. Their brand of "respectability" is just like those dirty movies: it makes a lie of the truth and of the beauty in all of us. I think we beat it ourselves and, in a way, I feel sorry for those who live with it—no matter what they tried to do to us or what they'll try to do to Jason with their numbed senses and deadened souls. Because you want to know what they'll never really understand? The one thing they can't feel so they fill the Outdoor every Saturday night? Love—that is what they can't feel, understand. And it's a real shame, but I guess that's the way it goes.

. . . DADDY PICKS UP the stick and then it's fighting fast against nothing. He says, Jason, stop crying. We're going to eat these. We gotta eat. So I go back in the trees and it's O.K. then, like when the stars are all over and I can feel myself. I know they are all right because I go back later with just the trees making the talking noise and then I see them—and they see me. Both of us are real quiet but they gotta keep moving to be still like me. I have the trees but they have the brightfast wetness that takes the leaves away. So they move all the time to stay in the same place I am. Cause I dont have to go against that fast wetness, all clear and bright. . . .

The Brass Bed

The convict lies on the narrow cot watching smoke from his cigarette swirl in and out of the sharp white shaft of moonlight. The pale light creates a hole in the darkness—a transparent square on the floor that seems to continue infinitely. It is pure like nothing else in the small cell. But the smoke disrupts the illusion and the convict is glad. Illusions are maddening here; the moonlight becomes real within those smokey swirls—a shaft of light from outside, trapped and imprisoned by its own frame of black and cold.

The convict turns and stares at the mesh of wires supporting the bunk above. The empty top bunk has always seemed absurdly useless, almost inhumane, here in solitary. Tonight it is ghostly visible, and for the first time in years the convict sees the wires bend down toward the center, sagging under the weight of another man. The convict cannot sleep with this stranger above him—under the weight of the possibility of something to be heard from another man: a story he might tell or just a voice to ease a certain empty aching in the breast, which the convict blames on the three packs of cigarettes he consumes each day. He is thinking that it is like when he was a boy and his older brother occupied the bunk above. His brother would occasionally tell him something in the dark, something about a secret cave or later about a canoe trip or still later about a girl he had met.

"Hey. You awake?" he whispers into the darkness.

His voice rasps with disuse and sounds a bit foolish, he thinks. The wires bounce and squeak above his head. He knows the other man is now staring at the gray ceiling. But there is no answer and the convict does not, at first, intend to continue.

"Want a smoke?" he asks.

"No. Thanks. I quit."

Just these absurd words, but his tone does not seem unfriendly. The convict takes it as a good sign and laughs.

"Hey, no reason to quit in here, friend. This here's solitary—or supposed to be. Meant to ask you about that."

The other man is silent for a moment.

"All right. Give me one."

The convict reaches for his cigarettes—six left. Payday tomorrow. He removes one and reaches over the top bunk. It is suddenly gone from his hand.

"Match?"

He takes the matches and lobs them onto the unseen man. He does not see the match explode, but for a second a yellow light fills the cell, overwhelming the white moonlight.

"What you in for?" the convict asks. He waits again for the answer.

"I'm paying for a brass bed."

The convict laughs but cuts it short, not meaning to offend. A spark glows inside him—he must talk. It will be bad if he doesn't.

"Where you from?"

"Up near Sherman."

"Hey, that's real nice country. I worked there once when I was younger. On a farm." No answer. "You live on a farm?"

"Yeah. A dream farm."

The spark glows. This is not going to be easy, the convict thinks, feels.

"What, whatya mean a dream farm? And what's this about paying for a brass bed?"

He hears the man above take a deep drag on the cigarette and exhale a smoky sigh.

"You know. A perfect dream farm. Dairy cows, potatoes, some

corn. A beautiful wife to give me sons—"

"You married?" the convict interrupts. "That's tough. I was all alone when I came in. Me and women, we were like oil and water. Can't understand them and they don't get me." No response. "I hear it's rough being a farmer these days."

"You could say that. I also worked in town—fixing cars. Working all the time. Seems strange not to be working now."

"You'll get used to it."

"Yes, I guess I will."

"In a way it's better here," the convict continues. He has not talked this much in years. "You get paid with cigarettes and toilet paper. Makes a helluva lot more sense than money."

"That's because there's no women here."

"What?"

"Women. Money. I worked and worked till I was set to collapse for them. For her. Money to buy her things. That's the way we lived. I worked and then I bought her things. That was it. Except she was always wanting more. But it felt so good to make her happy. You can put more money into your crops and they'll give you a better yield. But they can't love you back like a good woman."

"Yeah, I know what you mean," the convict says to keep it going.

The other man sighs. "She always wanted this big brass bed. Ever since that time in Chicago, in that fancy store and she saw it settin' there, gleaming and rich looking in them store lights. She really loved that bed. All she talked about for weeks. I felt real bad that I couldn't afford to buy it for her. You know how much a brass bed costs?"

"No idea." The convict tries to imagine just what a brass bed looks like; he has long since forgotten the arbitrary numbers that value things.

"Well, take my word for it—they're not cheap. And of course she wanted the biggest and best, like that one in Chicago. Not some cheap knockoff."

The convict expects more, but the story has abruptly stopped. "What you do? Break in and steal a brass bed?"

"Naw, I've never taken anything in my life. I just worked harder. From early morning till late at night. Pay off the farm bills, then save a little extra so I could buy her that bed. Late afternoon I'd quit the crops, eat a quick supper, and hurry into town to do some night work on cars. When I was finished, I'd stop at Jerry's for a beer or two. Be too tired to even say Pabst or Bud. They just put it in front of me when I come in. Then I'd drive home, and she'd be in bed—sometimes asleep but usually still awake. She never complained or asked questions."

The convict has lit another cigarette and inhales deeply.

"Yeah? Go on."

After a couple minutes of silence, "One Sunday I was going over the books and suddenly realized that if I held out on the new irrigation pipe till next season, I'd be able to afford the bed. All that day I was walking around the house smiling like the devil, and she got real suspicious and asked what I was up to. I'd just say, 'Oh, nothing,' until she could hardly stand it. It was a silly day. Funny how you like to remember things like that.

"Next day I quit the farm early and headed straight for town. But I didn't go to Ben's. Instead I went directly to my mother's place—right to the den and phoned that fancy store in Chicago. Really felt like something to be ordering a brass bed from a store such as that. They had marked it down some so I'd have no trouble paying for its delivery. That was a Monday. They told me it would come that Thursday.

"Those next two days were unbearable. I was so anxious to see the look on her face when the truck would come rolling up the drive and I'd come up (I was going to work on a pump all day to be near the house) and I'd yell "Honey, look at this!" as they would open the truck doors and there would be the brass bed she wanted so. I knew she wouldn't know what to say. She was like that—quiet, but you could tell from her eyes when she was happy. Her eyes would get big as two full moons. Seeing that was everything to me. Everything. I'd do anything to see her happy."

The convict is pleased with the story so far. He reaches up with another cigarette for the man, who takes it without comment.

"So the brass bed came Thursday?"

"Yes. It came, but Thursday didn't. Or Friday. It's all the same now—just the one, empty and endless day."

The convict wants to hear the ending; wants to hear what he knows happened because it has happened again and again since man walked out of Eden.

"Then something happened Wednesday," the convict prompted.

"Yes. That was Wednesday, then. The last Wednesday. I worked until five as usual. I kissed her goodbye with the same silly grin on my face and said I'd be home the usual time. Which is what I intended. But when I got to Ben's and began to work on this Chevy engine, I couldn't stand the suspense thinking how happy I was going to make her. Suddenly, I got this urge to see her and spend one last, beautiful night in our old wood-frame bed that had been our only bed since the wedding night.

"So, I washed up just as Ben stopped by to check things for the night. I told him that I felt sick, and he said that I should go home. I didn't stop at Jerry's and got home before eight. I was so excited I just ran wildly into the house calling her name. It was quiet. She didn't answer. I ran up the stairs. The door to our bedroom was shut. I carefully opened it and was about to whisper her name ... when I saw them. In our bed—my wife holding another man. I felt as if a machine suddenly sucked out all my living guts. They just stared at me stupidly. I vaguely realized that I knew him. We played football together in high school. But now he was something different: not a person at all—a disease of some sort, ugly and dangerous. He was acting silly, though, saying something and trying to get out from under the covers. I quietly stepped around the corner to the hall closet. I removed my shot-

gun carefully. It was loaded. I walked calmly back into the room. He...
it—the thing that should have been at that moment on the opposite
end of the universe—was watching me and trying to get his pants on.
He seemed to be moving incredibly fast, as if we did not exist in the
same time and place. She screamed, time stood still and the next moment now exists forever. I lifted the long, smooth barrel and aimed at
his chest."

The stranger has stopped talking; then, suddenly he leans over the
top bunk and looks down at the convict, his face grotesque in the pale
moonlight, and says, whispers, as if he needs to explain this:

"I killed him."

The face just as quickly disappears again. The convict is quiet. He is
satisfied with the story. It is what he expected, what he wanted to hear.
He imagines the strange woman now—this man's wife—in the shiny,
brass bed. But then he quickly thinks: No, she sold it. Got rid of it and
took the money instead.

"Did the brass bed come anyway?" asks the convict, as if commerce
could die along with a man's inner need for such things.

"Yes. It came on schedule. I know because they brought the papers
to the Elksburg jail for me to sign and pay for its delivery." He laughs
abruptly to emphasize the irony. "So I'm paying for a brass bed. I started
paying a long time ago when I began to love; then I believed I could
own it and I paid for its actual possession; and now I'm paying for believing in the possibility and the dream of a damned brass bed."

The convict turns toward the wall and closes his eyes, shutting out
the cold, white glow.

"One last question," he says. "Why are you here with me in solitary?"

The stranger rests a moment, his story at an end. Then, he sighs,
blowing smoke.

"The Warden says there're too many of us paying to get in. They're
overcrowded. Can't get a private room no more."

Yes, the convict thinks, he knew that, too. Now he will be able to sleep. He has heard the stranger's tale, and it is true because it is the first telling. Outside of the original absurd and unknowing physical actions, this is the first time the story has been told, created. It is the oldest of stories, but the convict now has proof that it is true and that, no matter how many have told it, the pain and the emptiness are not diffused and diluted among them through time, but rather each pays the full and dearest price, alone. Now, in this place, within these colorless walls, he will lose this story, lose all his stories, as the tales which were once repeated from generation to generation, through centuries immemorial, were forgotten within just one more generation when the people came down from the hills to live in the bright lights of the city.

A Change In Temperature

Paul walks through the smooth, white field, thirty feet from where my narrow skis break the virginal snow. I glance at him: a big man, clumsy in his Michigan snowshoes, holding the shotgun in his right hand. With his full, dark beard he seems the perfect mountain man. We have been friends a long time, and, now, as I kick and glide, I feel a warmth toward him. There was never any problem that he married the woman I had loved. I had been overseas a long time, and we all understood that time doesn't freeze solid like the pond below us. Time flows, ripples form, and flow back upon themselves. Last night's reunion glowed white hot—confused timelines, a past not as forgotten as time and memory had believed.

"Faster! Bet I can drop you in one shot!"

I hear this over the swish of my skis. To gain an extra moment, I do not snowplow but glide to a gradual stop. I have waxed just right—the kick and glide are perfect for the snow conditions. He is facing me, grinning, the gun under his arm pointed at the ground between us. This is no simple joke. Yes, I deserve it—it would be right. Resigned, I raise my poles in the air.

"If you really want to!" I yell back half jokingly.

He laughs and walks toward me. We continue in silence along the barbed-wire fence back toward the woods. I maintain an even diagonal stride, slowly, as he marches, gun in hand: a huge animal with awkward webbed feet.

"There's big wild turkeys back in there. Neighbor boy bagged one with deer shot."

"But you're using squirrel shot."

"Heck, I can still shoot me some tweety-birds."

He knows I dislike the indiscriminate shooting of animals. As does Joannie. I have never seen him hit anything, but today he will try extra hard to kill something.

Just inside the woods he shoots. The blast startles me. I look up as the target flies away, a few feathers falling gently to the snow.

"Damn," he says.

"Too bad," I say. "I love grouse. With a good wine, of course. You do have a good Chard just in case?

"Of course. Don't worry—you know how our tastes agree."

"Take football. The Pack."

"Baseball. The Brew Crew."

"Music. Haggard and Jones."

"Beer. Leinie's."

"Books. Hemingway. Art. Hopper."

He pauses. "Now you're getting a bit highbrow. What about women?"

I do not answer. I feel the shotgun's presence intensely as I contemplate what I would do had I the snowshoes, the gun, and Joan. Last night was nothing more than a temporal aberration, an anomaly. Yet somehow it changed everything. Even the winter landscape seems altered. I want to ski faster. It is torture to stay at his pace. The snow and the wax are rarely in such perfect harmony. Motion is ecstasy. The sun is burning the horizon through the trees; its orange and blue beauty also becomes too intense. Tall, straight trees rise from the snow; the bare limbs pierce the sky's changing colors. And the silence: I know if I stopped my skis, everything would become dead as outer space.

I stop and look at him, my friend's kind face. He stops and returns my look. The scene is still, but not dead. I forgot that we'd be breathing hard. And a wordless communication, which the words will destroy the truth of.

"I'm heading back," I stammer. "I have to go back." And immediately I know that I have forced the entire world—snow and trees and setting sun—to the point of annihilation.

"Go back? Why? I've got to bag a few tweety-birds. For the neighbor kid's fox traps, I get half the cut."

"The temperature's falling. My wax is too soft. I'm sticking." I stare stupidly into his eyes. "I'm heading back."

"I think you'd better hold on," he says. "I only got one shot off."

I perform an abrupt kick turn and begin a rigorous diagonal stride along the tracks I have just made. The wax *is* perfect. I feel everything—the snow, the wind: the situation, as if I fully expect to feel no more than the leafless trees in one short moment, before the next pole and stride.

His shot shatters the world. I am too close to miss, yet now I am skiing faster than ever. It is like I was born on skis. The first hills lie before me like huge, frozen ocean swells. Another explosion, cold and hollow, repeated by the snow-shrouded hills. I must confront her, all this: *What happens next? How can we—?*

She: *If I had known. If. . . .*

I am jumping on my skis, climbing the hill toward their home. It is a little colder now and the blue wax on the kicker grabs as I climb. *I forgot how great the tracking is in northern Wisconsin, but then it's been so long since I've even seen snow.* I can see the large A-frame, cathedral-like, against the sky.

Breathless, I glide to the door. With simple pressure of the pole tip, I release the bindings and the skis pop off. It feels like I have left behind a part of my body as I rush through the door like a madman.

She is standing in front of me, holding the baby. It's very warm inside; the sweat runs down my back.

"What's wrong?" she asks.

"Joannie—" I begin, and lose the words. It is as if they are outside in that lifeless yet life intensified world.

"What? Look wait a minute. I have to change Madison's diaper. One minute."

She quickly disappears into the baby's room. I begin to peel off my ski jacket, sweater, touring boots, socks. I feel at home. The baby is crying. The smell of a roast permeates the room. The Packer game is on T.V. Vin Scully announces that Marcol has just kicked a 35-yard field goal, the Pack going ahead 20-7.

"The Pack is back," she says, returning.

"Yeah. I hope so."

"Where's Paul? What is the matter anyway?"

I sit down on the couch overlooking the winter landscape from which I have become extricated: the hills, the ice-skating pond, the forest below. I look at her: large, smiling eyes; long dark hair. The ripples flow evenly.

"Nothing," I answer. "Paul's trying to shoot some tweety-birds. My wax wasn't right. No glide."

She looks at me like women do when you know that for a moment they understand the whole universe.

"Paul and I are so glad you could come up for the holidays." The words mask a truth—the reality. "We've missed you so."

"I missed you, both, too."

Our eyes meet.

I get it. It was just a minor glitch in a cosmic timeline.

"Paul will be home soon," I say, turning toward the T.V. Chicago has just fumbled. The horizon over the hills is the source of a blue world. The baby is quiet now. She gets up to go to the kitchen. The Pack wins, 27-14. I barely make out Paul walking up the hill.

"Here comes Paul," I yell to the kitchen.

"Tell him to leave any poor dead animal outside!"

Paul is my good friend. He'll have some bloody squirrel or sparrow to show us and he'll be happy to see us squirm in disgust. Then we'll have dinner; later we'll drink whiskey-sours and dance and get a little drunk. We'll be careful what we say, but not too careful. Perhaps, then, I'll try to tell them about it, about Nam, if the feeling is right. And when we arise tomorrow morning, we will feel closer, being three together in our bathrobes, and begin inventing sly and clever dialogue over breakfast, as the temperature outside rises imperceptibly above zero degrees.

["A CHANGE IN TEMPERATURE" was originally published in Pierian Spring literary magazine, Volume 6, Number 3, Summer 1981, Brandon, Manitoba, Canada.]

drunk. We'll be careful what we say, but not too careful. Perhaps, then, I'll try to tell them about it, about Nam, if the feeling is right. And when we arise tomorrow morning, we will feel closer, being three together in our bathrobes, and begin inventing sly and clever dialogue over breakfast, as the temperature outside rises imperceptibly above zero degrees.

["A CHANGE IN TEMPERATURE" was originally published in Pierian Spring literary magazine, Volume 6, Number 3, Summer 1981, Brandon, Manitoba, Canada.]

A Winter Dream

Johnny glanced around the barroom. Two guys playing pool, otherwise mostly empty, except for the three-sided bar. Almost every seat there was taken. His eyes were still adjusting, having lost the endless streaming white roadside mural frozen in his head like a composite landscape. *Some human contact would be good.* He chose the last available seat next to the wall beside a gentleman who appeared to be in his sixties or thereabouts.

"Excuse me," he muttered and squeezed in between the heavy coats filling much of the leftover space. He felt the eyes of this neighbor upon him.

"You new to these parts?"

Johnny looked at the man. He had a stubble beard, hair disheveled by a knit cap that now threatened to fall from his coat pocket, and clear searching blue eyes.

"You could say that," he responded, looking around the bar as if he might recognize something. "Came through here once before. Long time ago."

"Time is relative."

They sat a moment in silence pondering the local's deep thought as Johnny awaited the attention of the bartender, a young lady with substantial midriff showing even at 10 degrees outside.

"What'll you have?" his bar mate asked.

"That's OK, I've got it."

"I insist," he said, and after a pause, "Good to see a new face around here."

"OK, thanks. All right," Johnny studied the tap, gave up and then eyed the glass door of a cold case. "What's a good IPA in Sherman, Wisconsin?"

"You're gonna want the Wall Eye Pee Eh."

"You're kidding me right?"

"I am not Sir. Wall Brewing Company right down Elksburg way. You into the hops?"

"You could say that."

"Try it, guaranteed. On me anyway. Janie! The Stranger will have a Wall Eye."

Janie turned and looked at Johnny, briefly studying his face. Johnny saw that she was somewhat dark complected, looked a bit Native American, her eyes bottomless in the momentary glance.

"Sure Ed." Otherwise expressionless.

"Thanks." Johnny lifted his glass and glanced at his bar mate who merely nodded. "To new friends."

Ed said nothing. After a few moments, Ed queried, "So you a traveling salesman or something?"

Johnny was not sure he wanted to discuss what brought him back to Sherman after all these years, besides the booking, and perhaps in the back of his road-weary mind a vague memory of a girl long ago.

"Got an invite."

"Yeah? From who?"

"Whom."

He assumed his grammatical correction bothered this new acquaintance as there was a moment lacking talk, just the raucous laughter mixed with cable sports T.V. and jukebox.

"You play?" Johnny looked at him sharply. Ed explained, "Calluses on your fingers. Mostly left hand."

"Nice one Sherlock. Yeah, a little."

"Well come up here boy and show us who you are."

The reference to the old Kristofferson song further startled and began to intrigue him.

"Why you Devil," in further reference to the song. "You of the body I take it?"

"Just a fan. These old boys," his hand waved over the surrounding bar mates, "They like that New-Country crap."

"Does not surprise me. But I'm sure they're good people."

"Oh they are, just don't talk politics."

"Wouldn't think of it.

Johnny felt like it was his turn to initiate. *After all he bought me this beer.*

"So I guess you could say I've been a traveling salesperson, town to town selling my songs." He laughed. "Man that sounded trite."

"And how's business?"

"Same as always. Live on the applause."

Ed thought that over a minute. "Well good luck with that. Was good meeting you but I gotta go."

"Let me buy the next round pardner."

"Thanks Stranger, but I've got to get back to it." He didn't say what "it" was and the Stranger didn't think it polite to ask.

"Well hope we meet again sometime Ed. Thanks for the brew, good one."

"Not a problem. And I have a feeling we'll meet again."

"Not unlikely, funny how the circle is a wheel," leaving him with a reference to Gene Clark.

He chuckled. "Can't remember if we said goodbye." Ah Steve Earle.

"Ha! Until then."

Bare-midriff Janie was looking at him seemingly waiting for the end of their pointless banter.

"Another?"

He was downing the last of his ale when the bar suddenly exploded with "Robbie!" like the old "Cheers" show when Norm entered the bar. He turned to look. It had been close to thirty years but Johnny recognized him, about his age, salt-and-pepper bearded but hadn't changed much.

"At ease, y'all," Robbie commanded before taking a seat that seemed to be waiting for him.

Johnny felt an immediate connection to a different moment in time so long ago. He decided to let it be, when Robbie looked right at him.

"Who's the Stranger?"

He could have reminded him and perhaps discovered something about Robbie's sister, but he was sort of enjoying being the Stranger.

"Just that," Johnny answered.

"Well howdy Stranger."

"Another?" Janie repeated, neither annoyed nor not.

"No, thanks Janie, I have a show to get ready for."

She didn't care, or at least didn't ask.

HE TURNED UP THE HEATING unit in the wall of the little cabin that was about as cold as outside. The camp was otherwise vacant except for a group of snowmobilers at a nearby cabin. He carefully placed his guitar against a chair about six feet from the heat and waited for it to become accustomed to its new environment and breathe again. He was not worried about its resilience; it had seen many such places.

He sat down at the small table that the cabin provided and carefully unwrapped the sandwich he bought at the old Medford's store, which hadn't changed much in thirty years. He popped the bottle cap off the Wall's ale he also purchased there, having liked its hoppy bitterness at his roadside stop. It was very cold from being in the back of the van, and he drank it down with the sandwich as the guitar warmed to the occasion. The song list was studied as usual, a routine he enacted without thinking as he had done at so many stops over the years.

What would be appropriate for this place? Does it call forth anything not part of the usual rundown, a song list which included a couple minor hits of his, mostly that others had recorded, some Hank, a potpourri of country and alt-country standards, and about a third of his newer songs that would be fresh to them?

A vision of the strange girl he'd met those many long years and miles ago entered his head; the night he had sung her part of a song he later finished. It seemed like yesterday in his mind. Remembering the words she had said to him about getting away from Sherman, something about going to the coasts, he knew that she would be long gone. Nevertheless he grabbed the guitar and carefully worked on the song, which he hadn't revisited in a long while.

It was rough and a bit long for tonight's venue he thought, but then a quick flash of memory: her face in the moonlight liking it after he had finished a fragment of its debut. He had told her it was called "Remember the Words That You Said." Why not? Folks like a verse with a minor chord, remembering Guy Clark once saying to him that you had to throw in a minor chord for folks to take it seriously. He finger picked it carefully for the first go-around as he recalled the words.

> *As the sun slowly slides by the willow*
> *And sets in a sky oh so red...*

He looked up the rest of the lyrics in the back pages of his notebook. *Yes*, he thought. *That will be appropriate. I'll sing it here and then put it away for good.*

THERE WAS A MOVIE THEATER at this location, he recalled, a World War II-era quonset hut re-purposed as a picture show some time after the big war. What he pulled alongside now was not that theater. He was told by the booker that it had been closed for years, but that a group of dedicated music-loving residents had brought it back to life as a performance venue. It was not unusual for him, a somewhat successful although mostly still unknown-to-most songwriter, to be booked at such a place, often called an "arts venue," these days. He didn't give it another thought as he stepped inside, guitar case in hand, and looked around for his official greeter.

Seeing no one that seemed to fit that job description, he turned to the girl at the box office.

"Hi, I'm Johnny Sandersen."

No reaction. Typical.

"I'm the act for tonight?"

"Oh right," the girl responded, looking down at a paper to make his identification official. "Hold on."

She disappeared into a back office. Then the door opened and a man appeared. It was Ed from the bar.

"I should have known," Johnny said.

Ed smiled wryly.

"Gotcha. Just having a little fun. I hang there a bit. Also had your itinerary from the front office."

"You sly devil, Kris's *Come up here boy and show us who you are.*"

"Welcome to the Sherman Center for the Arts. Hope that's not too pompous sounding for ya."

"Not at all. Love what you've done with the place."

"I know you spoke with our booker Annie," now all business. "She's here somewhere." Ed looked around like she might appear from behind some foyer artwork. "I'm just a volunteer, do sound and run the projector and so forth." As if that didn't sound important enough, he added, "I did recommend you to her, love your stuff."

"Well I'm honored. Thank you very much. Hope I won't disappoint."

Ed leaned in and covered his mouth like telling a secret. "Hey Johnny, look around you. Not exactly Music City USA here. We're the ones that are honored to have a songwriter of your caliber. So, let me show you the ropes... sure you're familiar with places like ours."

"Appreciate it. There are always surprises, and I like to limit them going into a show."

BY THE TIME HE HAD got himself acclimated and tuned up his guitar in the green room, he heard the crowd gathering in the small but now elegant hall. The sound check went smoothly, better than usual, *thank God a good sound man*, and he was of course confident in his material.

Pretty much just another town, another show. Which is why he found it strange that he felt a bit more nervous than usual for the past fifteen or so years since he left the band and went solo. There were enough fans who knew his background and his songs that it was usually not hard to fill such a room at a moderately priced gate. He had stopped thinking about "making it big" years ago, had become accepting of his level of success, even content with it.

He heard himself being introduced, all the usual stuff from his press kit. He walked out from behind the curtain to a warm if not enthusiastic applause. He nodded to the crowd, picked up his guitar, secured the strap around his neck, bent the mic up to his mouth to address the hall.

"Thanks so much. Wonderful to be here in Sherman, Wisconsin." He stopped and thought he'd go off script. Why not? "Actually this is my second time through your beautiful town, but the first was so long ago I barely remember, though I do recall some very nice folks here."

A smattering of applause.

He jumped right into one of his better known minor hits. Over the first verse he had become accustomed to listening for the applause of recognition, while the rest of his senses gauged the sound of the room. His guitar needed more, and as the audience clapped louder now than before, he motioned with a quick point to his Gibson and an up finger to Ed in the back to give it to him. He hit a chord and nodded approval.

"*Remember the Words!*" a voice, female, he clearly heard from the floor.

He was shocked, knocked completely off any kind of normal, but gathered himself and went into automatic composure mode, a wan smile and move to pretend to tune the guitar. Could she be here? He had doodled with the song various other places but had put it on the shelf years ago.

Alright. No time like the present to get through this one.

"Actually the last time I came through Sherman, Wisconsin, I was writing this one," he almost mumbled. Then looking up, "Many years ago. I recall trying a couple verses out on a poor defenseless soul." Self deprecation always good. He put his hand up above his eyes to shield the spotlights and see the crowd. "Glad someone remembers. So for all y'all, if I can remember the words, here's Remember the Words That You Said.

> *As the sun slowly slides by the willow*
> *And sets in a sky oh so red...*
> *I see that the willow is weeping*
> *And remember the words that you said*
> *I remember the words that you said*
>
> *The words that were different one morning*
> *When the sky held the sun's gracious dawn*
> *But last night the clouds hid hopeful stars*
> *And by morning they were gone*
> *And by morning you were gone.*
>
> *I could pack all my things and just drive off*
> *To a place your thoughts haven't touched*
> *But when I get there I'll find all of nothing*
> *Cause I wouldn't be leaving with much*

No I wouldn't be leaving with much.

But can I blame you that I am so lonesome
As the snow that now covers the ground
My soul would be a leaf that's wind blown
And falls without making a sound
It falls without making a sound

Broken moonlight that shines through the willow
Shatters dreams as I lie in our bed
But like a tree I'll have to stand lonely
And remember the words that you said
I'll remember the words that you said.

Moderate applause, about what he'd expect. He believed he heard one person clapping louder and longer than the ambient, but he couldn't be sure.

After that he went on automatic, playing his usual set list to a better-than-average appreciative audience. He thought he'd throw one Ed's way to break the routine to finish.

"I met someone who works here earlier, a great guy that's currently doing my sound, name of Ed." The applause was now louder than for his performance, a trick he had learned playing these small towns: acknowledge one of their own. But he also had been pondering the Kristofferson song Ed alluded to at the bar, thinking how positive and optimistic the song was, especially in regard to recent events in the world.

"Ed threw a line from this song in my direction earlier today. One of Kristofferson's early songs, To Beat the Devil[1]."

He began the talking intro, trying for Kris's laconic low drawl, *"It was wintertime in Nashville down on Music City Row, and I was looking for a place to get my self out of the cold."* He interrupted himself for a

---

1.   https://youtu.be/faF0wOsVucw

"talking to his guitar" joke: "They don't have any idea what real cold is down there in Nashville let me tell you." Again some laughter and applause for the reference to the hardy souls who lived this far north. He continued, *"To warm the frozen feeling that was eating at my soul, keep the chilly wind off my guitar.... I saw there was one old man sitting at the bar, and in the mirror I could see him watching me and my guitar. He said 'Come up here boy and show us who you are,' I said I'm dry and he bought me a beer..."*

He then sang the back and forth verses with the Devil, and finished with a message he wanted to leave the crowd with, one that Kris once left him with.

> *I was born a lonely singer, and I'm bound to die the same*
> *But I've got to feed the hunger in my soul*
> *And if I never have a nickel I won't ever die ashamed*
> *'Cause I don't believe that no one wants to know.*

Thinking that was perhaps a bit too preachy, he tried a closer he often used, Girl From the North Country[2], in which he mimicked the juxtaposed nasal delivery of Dylan against Johnny Cash's baritone. *"She was once a true love of mine."* Some laughter of recognition at the imitation and a nice round of applause.

"Thank you ladies and gentlemen!" and he made his exit with the usual applause and calls for an encore. He didn't do the "let 'em wait" thing but came right back out. But on the way back center stage he thought he'd do a switch from the planned minor hit of his they must have thought he'd forgotten to play.

The applause settled down as he bent over to pick up his metal slide in order to try to reproduce Jesse Ed Davis's bottleneck.

"Thanks again. This is a song that's been going through my head past day or so, not sure why, Gene Clark's One In a Hundred.[3] A smat-

---

2.   https://youtu.be/nOKYs4pMW3Q

3.   https://youtu.be/FcIZBK3KQh8

tering of applause for the recognition of a song by the former Byrd.

...Hear the bells ring, morning has come
Over the town the morning star fades in the dawn
Voices of time bringing surprise
Voices that sing in waking moments
To look in to life's eye

Aren't you glad it's another day
Look and tell
So you thought you would run away
But you know that way too well

Rhythms of rhyme
Seasons shall say
To look at a longer life now
A longer yesterday

Don't you come down
You know you're the one
Looking at tomorrow
Let your your troubles
Fade and fly
Into the sun

He'd done the song many times, but was surprised to note a welling up of a tear in his eyes as he immediately rose and moved to the side curtain, stopping momentarily to face the audience and raise his guitar by its neck above his head, shouting without the mic:

"Thanks again, y'all have been great. Good night!"

As he headed for stage right it felt suddenly and momentarily like the end of something.

HE GATHERED HIS GEAR together and left the green room, finding his way to the lobby, which held the usual group of customers, some of whom earnestly thanked him for his performance. Even a couple autographs on the CDs he'd left out front.

Then he heard her but did not see her. *As if the voice did not belong to the body.*

"Hey John, or Johnny now it seems. Glad to see you finished the song."

A quick look, just seeing the small crowd. Then lowering his eyes a bit he saw her, a woman sitting in a wheelchair. She seemed radiant in spite of her condition.

"Well. Is that you? Lisa was... is it?"

"It was and is."

"Wow. Been a long long time." Perhaps he had a song for such an occasion, but he had no words at that moment.

"Coffee?"

"Ah yeah. Sure. Sounds great. Just give me a minute to settle up."

He headed for the little office, similar to hundreds in which he'd done business end of night. He collected his due, and expressed his gratitude, but as he walked out of the small space felt a certain finality that he could not have defined.

"NICE SHOW, REALLY NICE."

"Thanks, so glad you were here to enjoy it."

"Really liked that last song."

"Ah the Gene Clark. One In a Hundred."

"Had a very uplifting feel."

"One of the reasons I played it, it felt right for today."

She stared at him unblinking.

"So, how do you stay so upbeat? You'd think after being in the business this long you'd be more cynical."

"Oh I have my days."

She smiled. She sat across from him at a small table at the Sherman Diner. He looked at her as if time had stopped. Maybe it had. Maybe the time between never existed, even if contrary to apparent evidence otherwise. He thought of how she had just navigated the corners and curbs of the street just two blocks down from the theater as if she had wings instead of a chair.

"So did you find what you were looking for?" Lisa inquired.

"Looking for? Oh, I don't know. I'm not sure what it was I was looking for. I mean, relative success at doing this, I suppose that's something, a bit more than I would have expected back then." He paused. "You?"

"Me? I'm still here obviously."

"Did you ever make it to the Coast?"

She grinned remembering their long-ago conversation.

"L.A. and I did not get along."

"No? Too big a sea?"

"Too much... an end."

He looked at her fully understanding.

"For me as well. I thought L.A. would be the place to make it. Like so many others it turned out to be a pricey way to fade to black."

"So we both end up here, in the middle of it all, in Sherman, Wisconsin?"

He thought about that.

"Well I haven't thought much about tomorrow."

"Sounds like you haven't changed much."

He grinned. *Ah yes I remember now that directness, that way of somehow knowing.* "I guess you may be right."

Moments, then trying not to be obvious. "So what do you do here in Sherman?"

"Bought a resort."

"Wow, a resort?"

"Yep. It had gone vacant and I thought that it could use some help. Sam Dawson Realty in town had plans to tear it down and turn it into condos. Couldn't let that happen. Sold the store and snatched the place. Was called The Birches. I kept the name."

He sat staring trying not to.

"How, I mean, do you manage?"

"Oh you mean this?" nodding to the chair.

"Well, I noticed how you can turn a corner on a dime, but, yeah."

"Have to tell you John... Johnny," smiling, "It's not been easy. But I get by with some help. Turns out I'm a pretty good manager. And judge of character."

"I do believe that."

"And since you've managed not to ask, a snowmobiling accident. Jeff wasn't so fortunate."

Johnny remembered, old images flashing in a currently useless mind.

"Jeff?"

"We got married."

He laughed and quickly stopped.

"You and Jeff. Wow, if my memory serves me well, which it often does not, I didn't see that coming."

"Turns out he was probably the best man I've known, that I knew well anyway, and he was here waiting when I returned from out West."

"I hope you had some time together. I'm so sorry. I remember him vaguely. He seemed to realize, long before I did, that the road was a dead end." *A long time before I did, will...*

"He was anchored for sure. He ran the store until the accident."

They sat silent a moment.

"Glad you finished the song."

"Oh, that one? Yeah. Hadn't sung it in quite awhile." He paused. "So glad you were there to hear it."

"God we were young and stupid," she said aimlessly and then as if to apologize, "I mean me anyway."

"Hey we all were."

"Where you staying?"

He looked out the window at the empty street, the cold night.

"Little place down the road. Ed or someone put me up there. It's adequate."

"Right, The Sundowner." She thought a moment. "Hey if you want I've got a slightly better cabin that's all yours. Heats up real fast, very comfy. Not my busy season."

There was no reason not to, no reason to even check his schedule knowing that until the summer at least, it was either... something... or back to a small empty bungalow in East Nashville.

AS THEY SAT NOW IN the kitchen of the main house of The Birches, the brandy warmed him as the ubiquitous summer sun had done the first time he had seen her magically appear near the diving raft that day so long ago.

"So are there any other regulars here?" he inquired looking out the kitchen window into the blue world of this, her new life.

"Just Ol' Bill we call him. He's one over from yours."

"Who's Ol' Bill?"

Lisa stared down at her brandy glass and then looked up at him. "We're not entirely sure. He knocked on the door a couple years ago. Said he was looking for Mary. Told him we didn't have a Mary. He insisted she lived here."

"A couple years ago?"

"Yep. He booked a cabin that night and has been here ever since. Writes checks that don't bounce. He's a little off, but who isn't," she giggled, and it reminded him of then, back when, back before whatever this was, is. "He pays, a bit less than the going rate, but he's a regular. I did a quick lookup. All I can find out is that he used to live in Ann

Arbor, Michigan, found him on the web in a University of Michigan directory. Seems he was a professor of literature there. Wrote a book about some Russian guy named... Turgenev?" She paused. "I heard someone say he owned a place across the lake once, but must have been a long time ago." Whirling around, "C'mon I'll show you my cool elevator that takes me to the second floor. Then I'll introduce you to your cabin; I turned up the heat earlier."

"Sounds great," he responded, the brandy swirling around his head in a calm, peaceful way.

She wheeled back and turned from the table in that swift almost unseen motion, then hesitated and deftly swirled back around.

"You know, I don't know what the future looks like for you. But if you ever get a bit road weary, I could use some... help... around here. I mean, I do alright, but—"

"I just might take you up on that."

HE WAS WORKING OUT a melody for some lyrics when there was a knock on the door. The sweet rush of Spring air off the ice-relinguished lake mercifully entered his cabin as he opened the door.

"Hey Bill!"

"Hello. I heard you playing."

"Oh, yeah, the window, finally open."

"I liked it."

"I'm glad. Just something I'm working on."

"Do you like Rod McKuen? Mary likes Rod McKuen. There's this one song..."

"Not that familiar. Wait." A words-and-melodies catalog scanned in his head. "Is this him?"

He began to work out the intro chords and began singing a song he remembered distantly.

I have been a rover[4]
I have walked alone
Hiked a hundred highways
Never found a home....

"That's it!" Bill hoarsely whispered. Johnny continued, remembering.

Still I ain't complainin'
I'm happy though you see
Once in a while along the way
Love's been good to me.

Johnny was astonished as he noticed a tear rolling down Bill's face.

"How 'bout a happier one?" he offered.

"No. That is the happy one."

"Good to know. Sorry I don't know more of his."

"That's OK. He's new on the scene. What about that one they've been playing all summer, Mary In the Morning[5]?"

Johnny didn't know whether to go along or go check with Lisa. *But who's to say it's not still 1967 somewhere?*

"How about this one," thinking he'd go with an uptempo from back then and began picking Polk Salad Annie[6].

Bill now seemed downcast and was silent. Johnny glanced at him, wondering what to do.

"Hey Bill, where is your Mary now?" he tried.

"They tell me she's gone."

"Well don't believe them." He didn't know why he said that. Bill looked up, hopeful.

"Oh I don't. I know she's here. She's always been here."

---

4. *https://youtu.be/OQLj9Qhu5gU*

5.   https://youtu.be/OQnuLlBGh20

6.   https://youtu.be/IBfMLmNjFn4

Johnny thought he'd change the subject.

"So I hear you're a lit guy. I used to be big into F. Scott."

Bill looked at him blankly. He mumbled, "The green light," then gazing downward, "I guess it brought me here too."

"Right," Johnny agreed, actually sort of understanding the crazy words he spoke, a flashback to those long-gone days working on a master's in American Lit.

"Listen, maybe I should get you back to your cabin. I'm working on a set list for the show tomorrow at the Center for the Arts. You know that I'm the regular opener there besides being the sort of handyman here, right?"

"Oh yes, of course. You're the man." He paused and added, "We just saw *Georgy Girl*[7] there."

"Would you like to come?"

"Well sure I'd love to." He paused. "I don't think I drive anymore, do I?"

"Don't worry, I got you. Thanks for stopping in Bill," as Johnny opened the door and walked the old man out into the welcoming sunset of Spring.

❧

"DOCTOR, WILLIAM'S ORGANS are failing"

—as his inner being hums still evenly, final brainwaves becoming one with the lake's afternoon swells....

On top of the hill inside the huge porch, sitting together on an old bed that overlooks the entire lake, there's a confluence of smells from the slightly musty porch, the pines in the breeze, and a touch of an aftershave sample tried earlier even without a need to shave. Dylan's Lay Lady Lay[8] comes softly into the space from the open door to the living room, the pedal steel floating gently as the incoming waves below. Through that door, within

---

7.   *https://youtu.be/AJaittLdfVo*

8.   *https://youtu.be/rWz88VY-FkA*

proper earshot, the sound of an occasional pan as her mom is putting up jam from the last of the season's raspberries. There hangs in the air a sense of my leaving, again. A suddenly cool late afternoon breeze comes through the screen porch. I try to explain that I need to finish college; she doesn't know if she'll even go to college she says. I don't want to leave. I don't want to leave now. But if I have to leave—
"Doctor I'm not getting a pulse——"
—this is a good place, a good place for leaving.

THE REVEREND LEE WAS wrapping up the lakeside service. "Lastly, we'd like to thank our local celebrity, Johnny Sandersen, and of course Lisa, for their selflessness in organizing this service to see to the proper last rights of Ol' Bill, as we've all come to know him,"

Johnny grinned at the local celebrity remark, *maybe there is something to being a big fish in a small pond.*

The Reverend continued, "So my understanding is that Johnny will wrap things up and then row out a bit so as to catch the west wind and scatter Bill's ashes across the beloved jewel of Hart Lake. Then you all are welcome to join us on the great porch of this wonderful old lodge for food and refreshments."

Johnny was ready with the tuning and began a gentle strum. "Here's a song by Mr. Bob Dylan in honor of another wayfaring stranger who was taken in by this good town, followed by one Bill always liked me to play for his long lost love, Mary, wherever she may be." He added unscripted glancing down at his finger placement, "I guess we all have a Mary."

> *I hear the ancient footsteps like the motion of the sea*[9]
> *Sometimes I turn, there's someone there*
> *Other times it's only me*

---

9. *https://youtu.be/q5fkoVAiudU*

I am hanging in the balance of the reality of man
Like every sparrow falling, like every grain of sand

Sensing a presence eclipsing the waning sun he looked up. The figure of Mr. Latimore from the Post Office stood above him.

"Thank you John, and Lisa, for doing this. It means a lot to all of us."

John smiled and nodded. Lisa said, "George, I believe Emma went up to the house, why don't you join her."

"Yes. Thanks. I just wanted to thank both of you."

"Our pleasure. I'm glad... Emma is doing better," responded Lisa, who knows everything about everyone in town.

"Yes, so am I," Mr. Latimore responded looking around toward the main house. "See you up the hill."

Johnny realized that he was losing his audience to the food and drink. *That is as it should be, all is as it should be.* He decided to save his acoustically re-worked version of Hendrix's The Wind Cries Mary for an upcoming Saturday night at the Center.

Lisa waited lakeside with the box of ashes. He knelt on one knee as had become natural to be at her physical level, she being so much above him in so many other ways. Their eyes met. He took the box from her in silence.

Then, as he steadied the rowboat to board, he turned back and said, "Let's get married."

"Let's," she replied.

Johnny gently placed the box containing Ol' Bill on the bottom ribbing of the wood Thompson boat, and rowed out to the middle of the lake, the small swells slapping against the sides keeping a gentle rhythm with the oars, while the entire lake echoed a loon's pure and mournful tones.

The Family Plot

I look out the window. I sit at my usual place on the couch, just far enough from the window so that it isn't so obvious when I glance outward. I can just barely see the iron-gated corner of the cemetery plot. Surrounding it are other medical buildings, all identical and all made to look like a developer's idea of some long-gone architecture, incorporating silly faux artifacts, not with any semblance of scale, all of which contribute to a disturbing effect opposite that to which they are supposedly meant to elicit.

Schaff told me the story once. The developer had made a deal when they bought the old farm and homestead to build this medical park. The deal was: do whatever you are going to do, but leave the family plot. Officially memorialize it. Don't mess with the family plot, except to trim the lawn. And install a nice, approved iron fence and gate to enclose it forever and keep it safe from whatever havoc you're about to unleash. And it is to be so kept and maintained, the paper to which the developer agreed states.

Schaff is telling me again how intelligent I am. Not sure how he knows this. The guy doesn't read. Never heard of Walker Percy; had to give him a copy of *Love In the Ruins,* making sure to tell him it cost less than a buck so he could accept it. Next visit he was excited as he had discovered that Percy had been an inmate in a sanatorium in upstate New York at which he knew a staff member. Doubt he read the book. Might be a good thing, might think I'm implying I have something in common with the protagonist. You know how guys like Schaff think.

I stare out the window, answering something to Schaff to keep it going. Yeah I know I'm intelligent but sometimes that makes it worse, doesn't it? I ask to make him continue. I stare through the window. *The parson is giving last rights, his Bible open to the verse, the family and friends from neighboring farms circled 'round.*

Schaff is highly educated in his field, but he is not cultured in any popular sense. He didn't even know who Bob Dylan was until he won the Nobel Prize. He was so happy with himself when he could tell me that he heard a song by the Byrds that was written by Dylan. The song was My Back Pages[1]. It proved to him that he was indeed in touch with contemporary culture. I was so much older then I'm younger than that now. Maybe not so much.

The woman who is being laid to rest has died young. There's some whimpering from the children, but the adults, who have come from all the surrounding farms, just look down at the freshly dug plot. The year of our Lord 1918 has taken its toll and this get-together is already far from un-common.

Samuel, Schaff blurts out even though I've told him to call me Sam. What do you think about that?

I believe I had heard something about the same old thing. I just couldn't quite remember which thing it was. Yes I respond automatically now, I know what you're saying. I need to make decisions. I need to move forward.

Yes, he went on. Losing a loved one is very hard. This isn't something one recovers from immediately.

"Death is only a state in which the others are left." Faulkner whispers in my head.

And I'm there again. I dig the hole in the forest floor, chopping through fern and balsam roots, roots which the ashes in the nearby plots under random field stones have nourished, as the spade digs through the sandy loam. My little girl watches, her face a mix of sadness, interest, astonishment, and perhaps even pity. She is only 10. The

---

1.   https://youtu.be/OZwncQfvaKk

stereo is heard through the woods, from the cabin some 30 feet away, Emmylou Harris is singing *It don't matter where you bury me, I'll be home and I'll be free...* The box of ashes feels strangely light in my hands. It doesn't quite fit the hole. I believe I'm beginning to wail. I set the box down again. Tears are flying as I dig furiously at the ground with my hands. *All my sins be washed away* she sings. My little girl looks on, I don't know if she is crying, I don't think so. It is all just too brutal.

Between grief and nothing I will take grief.

In an attempt to evict Faulkner, together with memory, from my head I glance back out the window.

The parson stands straight as someone who hasn't been working the fields, and is reading from the Bible. It's a beautiful day in early fall. The father fidgets with the brim of his hat, not even realizing that he's worrying about a field that is waiting his attention. The young daughter is just beyond my view, beyond the edge of the window. At least I believe that's why I can't see her.

So what's this about the land? A cottage on a lake, what, in northern Wisconsin is it?

A cottage. OK doc, listen up. A *cottage* is what they call it where you go in north Ontario. That picture above your head of you fly fishing, taken in the Adirondacks? Up there they call it a *camp*. I have a *cabin*. A good-sized well-constructed cabin with electric, running water and all, but in Wisconsin it's called a cabin.

He continues as that little outburst explodes in my head. Cleveland is a ways from there. I know it means a lot to you, but it has become a burden, hasn't it? Schaff is going on about an actual concern I've expressed, a nagging worry—the land that was (and always is) my parents' and my grandparents' before that, and which is now mine, now almost a century in the family. It needs much attention. In my younger days it was my safe spot, as it was through all those corporate years.

And the lake. My lake dream, that would be something to make Schaff salivate: a recurring dream I'm having of late, where I find our lake suddenly half filled in and grown over with brush and trees so that I can't see the other side. *Damn Geography degree that did me no good.* But a flash of memory, in one class something about how a lake gradually becomes, well, not a lake. The textbook called it *eutrophication.* Our lake is spring fed, unlike the glacially carved lakes of Sherman's famous chain of lakes. An outlet from our lake then runs into and feeds those other carved-out channels. But beavers have been damming up the outlet for years. Short term, the lake level rises taking with it some great white pines, hundreds of years old, from along our shoreline. I have a persistent fear the damming of the outlet will seal off the springs, as their natural function in the scheme of things is gone. The lake will then die, becoming terrestrial, probably several lifetimes after I'm gone—but happening now, sped up in my dreams. Schaff would actually be very interested in this on at least two fronts. But yeah... no.

You said your financial person suggested you sell it? Schaff is still interrogating so I respond.

Yes Doc Schaffton. I have a money guy. He was my parents' guy. Now he's my guy. I don't want this guy, and that may become a moot point. He wants me to sell it, the land, the cabin. My past. *My was, and my is.* When the guy looks at me, he sees it all as dollar signs in the positive column of the ledger. And he has a point.

Schaff is still talking. When you're young there are, or seem to be, infinite paths. When you get (pause) older, there are far fewer, due to time and circumstance.

Wow, did Schaff just say something semi-profound?

Thought you were supposed to prop me up? Schaff chuckles softly at this, which is something. So right, you're dead on with that one. I pause. *There are perhaps, probably, in some ways, more paths, one is just denied the freedom to see them.*

I respond to his followup. My novel? Ah, been working on it when I can, but no one reads anymore, just tweets. Perhaps that's Hemingway's fault, we could blame him, always a good target. He doesn't get the joke of course, and I don't bother.

He's now asking about my other current activity as a would-be music promoter. Yes, but my top guy, Johnny Sandersen, a former big-time Music City songwriter, is on the downside of his career playing small venues, like the Arts Center in Sherman, you know, the town near my place? My cut doesn't pay the bills.

But Schaff can't do anything about money problems. So what am I doing here? We stop a moment and everything becomes still, just an empty room with only the faint smell of old books. Schaff starts up again, now he's on me again about seeing a doctor, a real one.

A quick glance sidelong back out the window.

The father is leading a parade of his several children, all different ages, back to the homestead. His son, who is already taller than he, follows close behind. The father quickly turns and says something to the son, which stops the line momentarily.

So I want you to think about that. The non-specific and vapid comment from Schaff forces me unwillingly back into his office. He sits as any wise man sits, in his winged-back, well-cushioned chair. There's the usual pile of books on the floor. Has he been researching my "case" or is it just a prop?

I have no answers for Schaff and he has no answers for me.

The film reverses a few frames and the lens zooms in on the father talking to his son. You are the oldest. You are a man now. You know everything I know about the farm. He stops and stares into the blank and unknowing expression of his son, then turns around and again begins to lead the others back toward the homestead.

Any thoughts of doing harm to yourself?

Schaff feeds me that well-worn mandatory closing line. Are we done already? If I say anything but No to this ritualistic question things would get complicated, others become involved, there would be no escape. No, I respond as usual. I believe I'm probably being truthful. He looks at his watch. Then he says, I have to talk to you. I'm semi-retired and I can't keep seeing you anymore at the rate... your insurance is allowing. We can work something out though he adds like a true salesman.

Oh, I see. I stand up. Thank you. It's been enlightening. I'll think about it. I pause. But I think we're probably done. I tell him I think he's helped me, that I'm much better. He looks pleased at that, which is all I can ask for.

Maybe we can get a beer sometime, I joke as I shake his hand and turn my back on another little chapter of my life.

I pass through the double glass doors and enter the white winter cold, which slaps my face and feels good in the nostrils and lungs. I take a glance around at the building. *Was I ever even here?* I begin to walk back toward my ancient Ford pickup, and I stop. I turn and begin to walk through the foot-deep snow around the massive building as I never have done before.

And I am there.

Beside the wrought iron fence I can read the wind-worn engravings on the headstones. The largest two of seven: Emma Knudsen, Died September 1918. Beside her: Merle Knudsen, Died December 1918. And there, in this now forsaken spot where no one visits, disappearing into the distance, are the footprints in the snow.

Epilogue: Peaceful Waters

(After John Prine's Lake Marie[1])

THE ONE YOUNG MAN SAID to the other young man, both of whose ancestors had lived in this place for centuries, what shall we name them? They knew little of the pale-faced men, had seen them once in a far-off village. They looked down at the babies, both girls, both lacking in color other than a rosy hue, one a little larger than the other. They were in a basket of sorts, lined only with newspaper. The paper was wet, as were they. The two finders looked at each other. The babies had nothing else and no one else, so they needed at least to be named.

One of the men held the larger baby while the other looked over pieces of the newspaper. A picture appeared in the wet paper of two girls playing some sort of game. They looked like shadows in the black-and-white, flat, wet world. Below the picture were letters in English that they supposed were the girls' names. The two tried to sound out the names in Algonquian as they saw and interpreted the characters.

It also so happened, as they had been scouting for fresh fishing grounds, that they found two lakes nearby, one larger than the other, the smaller one unseen at first being off their well-worn foot path. Each of the finders held a baby as they looked out from the shore, standing by the peaceful waters. The babies and the lakes became one, and they named the lakes by the same names they had named the babies. They were in a hurry to get the infants to their village and the women, who would know what to do.

---

1. *https://youtu.be/te7x8s9P4U8*

Much later, when the pale-faced people came and claimed the land around the lakes as their own, they were told the names of the lakes by a friendly Ojibwe, who explained that they were female names. The closest the names sounded to the newcomers were Marie and Elizabeth (no one really knows what was printed and interpreted from the paper by the original two finders of the babies, nor what happened to the finders so many years before) and so the two nearby lakes were named Lake Elizabeth and Lake Marie, Elizabeth the larger of the two.

WE LEAVE THE MEMORIAL Day-crowded campground at Lake Marie arguing about something, and we're like that almost all the way to Canada. That's nothing new. I thought the camping at Lakes Marie and Elizabeth would bring back those peaceful times, but apparently my distinct but now distant memories, her wind-blown hair, brats sizzlin' on the grill—man they was sizzlin'—peaceful waters, are merely my own. So we head north, with no destination other than a vague idea about searching for Neil Young's hometown after the radio had played Thrasher[2] one day. But mainly we're looking to catch some fish, or save our marriage, whichever is easier, or comes first. The trip is at least a reprieve of sorts, and things get better as we make camp on the chilly Canadian north shore of Superior.

There are others camped nearby but we have enough space and supplies. Louie Louie[3] is playing softly on the radio. Matter of fact, the day has turned out pretty nicely, we've actually had a good day. She is humming Louie Louie as she falls asleep in my arms.

Ah baby, we got to go now.

---

2. *https://youtu.be/HOgSTD7Kjrw*

3.   *https://youtu.be/xKt75jUuKJY*

NOW BACK AT LAKE MARIE, alone, things seem upside down. I finish making camp as the truck's satellite radio plays some crap new country. I go to fill my containers; the rusty pump pours as words from a long-gone past try to replace the radio waves... "the water tastes funny when you're far from your home, but it's only the thirsty that hunger to roam...."

Someone screams.

A dog barks.

The police come.

Others, lots of them, parking exhaust-spewing cars along the state forest road and parking area. A body, no two, have been found, naked someone says, mutilated, the faces cut beyond recognition. Everything is pitch black, bright stabbing flashlights, screaming.

Shadows. Like blood looks on a black and white TV screen.

Being here at our spot on Lake Marie tonight, well, it just feels like I, we, all the love that we shared, it was slammed, slammed by a north wind against the banks of Lake Marie.

Ah baby, we got to go now.

About the Author

As a kid in the back seat, making the long trek from Buffalo to the grandparents' cabin in northern Wisconsin, Will loved the small towns. Majoring in Geography, it was in the lit classes where he began to live in places such as Winesburg, Yoknapatawpha, Horton Bay, Brewer. Some of these chapters were written in those early days, and some recently to complete the mosaic. The themes are well-trod -- home and rootlessness; love, longing and loss; and the individual's place in the natural world, in his or her community, as well as within his or her own interior self. Will James Harnack has worn many hats, writer, house painter, magazine and corporate editor, historic preservation commissioner, webmaster, music concert producer, son, husband, father, and hopes for time for much more.